"Brennan has written an alternate reality in the Cold War. An account of two Soviet cosmonauts on a dangerous mission to the moon becomes, in Brennan's hands, a character study about ambition, luck, and courage from the halcyon days of the space race. As with his earlier book on Gagarin, *Public Loneliness*, Brennan has an uncanny ability to dig deeper into the world of the spacefarer in a way that is rare, satisfying, and often unsettling. A great addition to his canon."

> — **Asif A. Siddiqi, author, *The Red Rockets' Glare: Spaceflight and the Russian Imagination, 1857–1957***

PRAISE FOR ALONE ON THE MOON

"Gerald Brennan is the poet laureate of the desolation of space, a master of capturing it not as the operatic backdrop of movie science fiction, but as the darkly oppressive deadly void between worlds. *Alone on the Moon* is Brennan in peak form—it's *Apollo 13* minus Hollywood, a very human exploration of an alternate history moon mission...right up to its nail-biting conclusion."

> — **David Hitt, author, *Homesteading Space: The Skylab Story***

OTHER BOOKS IN THE SERIES

INFINITE BLUES

"Employing the scrupulous detail of classic technothrillers alongside James-Ellroy-esque reality-scrambling and a fractal elegance that recalls the work of Agustín Fernández Mallo, *Infinite Blues* plays out against the perilous backdrop of a reimagined Cold War in which the conquest of space has been undertaken neither in peace nor for all mankind."

— **Martin Seay, author, *The Mirror Thief***

ISLAND OF CLOUDS

"Brennan is clearly having a ball here, reimagining the what-ifs and might-have-beens from the golden age of space exploration. His research, passion, authenticity, and exuberant writing all bring the implausible to life-- man and machine, earth and moon. For fans of Andy Weir's *The Martian*, NASA's Apollo era, *2001: A Space Odyssey*, the 60s and 70s, *Star Trek*, and anything by Bradbury, Bukowski or Le Guin. Speculative sci-fi at its finest."

— **Neal Thompson, author, *Light this Candle: The Life and Times of Alan Shepard, America's First Spaceman***

ALONE ON THE MOON

A SOVIET LUNAR ODYSSEY

GERALD BRENNAN

KAY:
ENJOY THE
VOYAGE!!!...

25 JUL 22

Other titles in the series:

Zero Phase: Apollo 13 on the Moon

Public Loneliness: Yuri Gagarin's Circumlunar Flight

Island of Clouds: The Great 1972 Venus Flyby

Infinite Blues: A Cold War Fever Dream

ALONE ON THE MOON

A SOVIET LUNAR ODYSSEY

PART OF THE ALTERED SPACE SERIES

GERALD BRENNAN

TORTOISE BOOKS
CHICAGO, IL

FIRST EDITION, MAY, 2022

Copyright © 2022 by Gerald D. Brennan III

All rights reserved under International and Pan-American Copyright
Convention
Published in the United States by Tortoise Books

www.tortoisebooks.com

ASIN: B09HX4JDWC
ISBN-13: 978-1-948954-65-5

Front Cover: AS15-96-13085, A view featuring the Moon's "Southern Sea".
Image credit: National Aeronautics and Space Administration. Scanning
credit: Kipp Teague

Interior Images: Detail from N1-L3 line drawing, ©2022 Alexander
Shliadinsky. Used with permission.

Soyuz 7K-OK line drawing, ©2022 Michael J. Mackowski. Used with
permission.

Tortoise Books Logo Copyright ©2022 by Tortoise Books. Original artwork
by Rachele O'Hare.

With eternal gratitude to Giano Cromley for climbing aboard an untested craft and embarking on a voyage into the unknown. Your guidance and friendship have been indispensable.

"'The essence of man,' Budach said, chewing slowly, 'lies in his astonishing ability to get used to anything. There's nothing in nature that man could not learn to live with. Neither horse nor dog nor mouse has this property. Probably God, as he was creating man, guessed the torments he was condemning him to and gave him an enormous reserve of strength and patience.'"

– Arkady and Boris Strugatsky, *Hard to be a God*

Golden

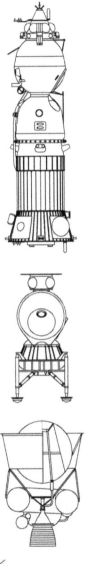

© А.Шлядинский.

We cannot see anything through the windows of our spacecraft.

We are coasting through cosmic space, between the earth and moon. One might expect glorious vistas: the cloud-mottled blue of our home, the intricately pockmarked gray of our destination. But our orientation's wrong for that. The nose of the spaceship is pointed at the moon, and the whole assembly's spinning slowly about the roll axis, like a pig roasting on a spit. So the various portholes are taking their turns pointing at the blinding sun, or off into the blackness of space.

And it is indeed black. For in this sun-soaked place, the pupils contract enough that starlight is not visible to the naked eye. So: no panoramas of the galaxy spread out before us; we cannot even see individual stars, except by placing covers on the portholes and looking through the periscope.

Still, Leonov—or Blondie, as Yuri used to call him, with a familiarity I never had—has retrieved a pad of paper, an artist's sketchpad, and is pulling out charcoal looking to create…what? A work of art? Here, floating in space, awkwardly holding everything with no gravity to keep it in place, he is going to create a masterpiece?

"We can't see anything," I point out. "What are you going to draw? You're going to look through the periscope to see one single star? One crater on the moon?"

"We can see the interior."

"You could have drawn that back on earth. Spent some extra time in the training mockup."

He allows me a slender smile: a thin crescent, swiftly waning. "We could have done a lot of things back on earth, Boris."

He struggles to get the drawing pad in place, pressed between wrist and thigh; when that fails to satisfy he abandons it for another tactic, holding the pad tightly in one hand and sketching loosely with the other. Trying to sketch loosely. I drift around to get out of his way, and shake my weightless head. Add a noise of disdain.

"It feels different up here," he adds. "The light is different."

"You're not worried?"

"About the mission?" A weightless nod towards the unseen moon, on which he's scheduled to leave humanity's first footprints. All alone.

"About what people will think. If anything goes wrong. That you were distracted by...frivolities."

"Nothing's going to go wrong."

"You'll jinx us, by saying that."

"I've sketched up here before, you know." Another attempt at a line of charcoal. It does not look successful. Nevertheless, he continues. "On Sunrise-2. I made four quick sketches right after my spacewalk, while the memories were still fresh."

"Four sketches."

"It was quite an experience! To be the first one out there, floating alone in cosmic space..." His eyes grow distant. He was indeed the first one out there; Yuri and the others were up here first, to be sure, but they had all still been cocooned in the metal shells of their spaceships. He was the first to get out there alone, to be able to look this way or that and see, either way, the infinite blackness. A swimmer in the cosmic ocean. A more thrilling first than Yuri's...it doesn't seem fair that he should get yet another.

Still: "Four sketches."

"There was a lot to remember! The spacecraft was bathed in this...blinding white golden light. Impossible to capture with charcoal, unfortunately. I tried to get it right in my paintings. But I'm not sure it's ever been as vivid as it is in my memories..."

"I have a memory. Of you talking to Sergei Pavlovich." Korolev, the Chief Designer. "That big party, at OKB-1, right before he went to the hospital for the first time. I was standing behind you as you talked to him."

"You were spying on me."

"Not an uncommon preoccupation, you must admit. I heard you telling him about the flight. You said, very distinctly, that you had made three sketches."

Floating, our faces are fuller than normal: blood unhindered by gravity, puffing up the face and eyes. Do I see an extra red flush of shame? An unfamiliar emotion for the golden man, the people's idol...

He looks away.

I continue: "What is the point? Making a big story bigger. What is the need? To put one more sketch on exhibit? To give away one more keepsake? Come to think of it, how do we know you've drawn anything in space? If you're having so much trouble with it now..."

"You could let me have some fun, at least." He turns his attention back to the sketchpad. Still, he allows me a fuller smile this time, punctuated by a shake of the head—a quick rotation about the yaw axis, initiated and reversed and arrested.

•••

We were not supposed to be crewmembers for this, the greatest mission. We were not supposed to be crewmembers—but then came the accident.

We have never been friends. Is that his fault or mine? Who can say. He says every person is unique, so every relationship is unique; he is always talking about crew compatibility, as if he's a wine drinker searching through proper pairings. Whereas I feel like everyone who mentions these things is looking for a sanitized reason to express their prejudices.

I retrieve my dinner from the storage area. A can of beef tongue and a packet of black bread. I pull myself through the interior hatch and into the cramped descent module so I can eat in peace. Lips tight on my false front teeth: frustrating memories.

"Dining alone?" he calls through the open hatch.

"I'm letting you have your fun."

"If we eat together enough, maybe we'll be friends. Like the saying goes: wait and be patient. You'll love your wife eventually."

"There are two of us up here, and two modules. It seems like a satisfactory arrangement." I open the beef and start eating: fatty and salty and all mine.

He floats in nevertheless, pad and charcoal in hand. "I know what it was. Why it was easier last time. I was strapped in." A full smile now, a cursed smile. "There are two seats in here. It seems like a satisfactory arrangement."

My meal floats in front of me, parked in empty space in the middle of the module; I have to shepherd it out of the way to make room for the golden boy. I sigh so he knows it's an effort.

"Beef?" he says, with a nod at the tin. "You didn't want the sausage?"

"I like the beef." Was it an innocuous question? Or his way of probing about dietary restrictions—that word, the other half of me, the one that means all of me to some: Jew. "We have a broadcast coming up, do we not?"

"We do indeed. We should pretend to be friends, for the sake of socialist fraternity."

"I'm a cosmonaut, not an actor. One flighty creative type is quite enough for a crew."

"We should pretend to be friends." He takes his place, oblivious to my discomfort.

"As long as we don't have to share a fraternal kiss."

"We will be brothers, in a sense. Once this is over." Strapped in now, everything is easier for him; he starts fresh with a black circle, the empty void of the porthole. "I can show the camera a sketch or two. So people on Earth know I've drawn something in space."

"There will still be doubters. Remember after your space-walk? The Americans spread those rumors…"

He purses his lips, shakes his head. "As if we'd fake all that."

"There are people who will doubt we're up here, even."

"We can prove it to them. Turn the spacecraft sideways. Show them the earth and the moon."

"They will say we're on a set at Mosfilm."

"We will be floating."

"A clever series of cuts, they'll say. Footage from the studio, and film from a training flight on a Tupolev."

"We can prove it to them." His charcoal hand flies across the paper, laying down shapes. Outlines of panels and hatches. Light and loose and carefree.

•••

I retrieve the television camera from the storage locker. Our first broadcast will be starting soon. This is the one task we haven't rehearsed. And yet: important, to the powers-that-be.

"What should I show them?" I ask Leonov. Whatever issues we've had, he's still the commander.

"We'll talk to Control about showing the earth and the moon. It won't cost much propellant, to do it once."

"And inside the spacecraft?"

"I have the sketches."

"They'll think you did them on the ground."

"I can pretend I'm touching one up for the camera."

More dishonesty. "All right. The Alexei Leonov Show. Starring the greatest cosmonaut, artist, and all-around human being of our time, with the earth and the moon in supporting roles."

"We can take turns on camera, Boris!"

"Very well."

"You're a part of this, too. Enjoy it." His weightless eyes make him look Oriental, call to mind the old musings about whether Russians are Europeans or Asians. And with both of us born in Siberia...

"Yes, sir." I hand off the camera.

A radio voice in the headset: Komarov. "Golden Eagle..." (Our call sign, stolen from East-4.) "...Golden Eagle, this is Control. Come in, over."

"Control, Golden Eagle. Go ahead, over."

The radio waves take their time through cosmic space; the slight delay reminds us the distance is real. "Golden Eagle, please turn on your camera so we can confirm receipt of signal."

"Very well...just a moment." To me he nods. "Go into the orbital module. We can have you do...somersaults or something."

I float through the hatch and into the roomier space. Somersaults. Circus tricks for the masses.

Again, Komarov: "Golden Eagle, Control. We have no signal. Is the camera on?"

"Control, here you go. Over." He flips the switch and I can see the red light. All those eyes.

Or maybe not yet. "Golden Eagle, Control. We are barely getting an image. Please adjust your connections. Over."

"Control, Golden Eagle. The broadcast is starting in five minutes, correct?"

"Affirmative, Golden Eagle."

"Let me reposition the spacecraft stack. Our instruments are showing 96% on propellant. We'd like to show them something out the windows. Stand by." He straps in loosely.

"Do you need me to..." I gesture towards the other seat.

"You'll be fine." He smiles. "The walls are padded."

"Just like the asylum," I mutter.

His hand twitches on the controller and we hear thruster noise transmitted through the frame of the spacecraft and suddenly I feel like I'm rotating slowly, though it's just that the ship has stopped. One side swings gently towards me; I raise a hand to push off the padding.

But he's not paying attention, just checking the portholes for home and destination. "There we go." He sounds, as usual, quite pleased with himself. "Control, Golden Eagle, we have repositioned. Over." Then to me: "What did you say?"

"It's like…"

Ground crackles in. "Golden Eagle, we have lost your television signal entirely. Please repoint your antenna to angle nine-zero degrees, elevation one-five degrees. Over."

"Control, stand by." Leonov adjusts the directional controls.

I shake my head. "You're going to fly the whole mission yourself?"

He grins. "Just the important parts."

"Ahh. So picking you up after you lift off from the moon…apparently it's not important?"

"All right. The challenging parts." His grin grows wider. Then to ground: "Control, Golden Eagle. How is that, over?"

After the delay: "Where is your camera pointing? We cannot see much. Over."

The camera has, in fact, floated towards the bulkhead in the descent module; even if it's transmitting perfectly, it can't be showing much. I pull my head and arms through the hatch, grab it before Leonov can, and point it straight at him. "Control, I've got him in my gunsights. Over."

"Attacked by a madman," he says, nonchalant. "Nothing I haven't lived through already."

And nothing we want to talk about on the air. Shame floods my face. In my mind, the flicker of snapshots: the policeman's uniform, the flash of the muzzle, the limousine windows shattering, the crowd screaming. I hadn't even been thinking of that...

"Golden Eagle, he looks like a blurry ghost. Try adjusting again. Over."

Leonov scans the antenna knobs but does nothing. "Control, maybe the problem is on your end. Have you tried putting aluminum foil on your antennas? My wife swears by that."

So typical of Leonov: claiming the problem is elsewhere. But his delivery's warm enough that after the delay I hear laughter on the other end. I remember the years of shortage before I flew, the years when foil was a luxury. "Not everyone has access to the special stores," I remind him.

"Let's not talk about the special stores," he says. "We don't know who's listening."

After the delay, Komarov crackles: "The country will be listening! The country, and the world. We haven't formally announced the plan for the landing, but the rumors are..." (Static.) "...so please be..." (The rest is lost.)

"Please repeat, Control." Leonov grabs the camera from me and nods towards the module. "Go," he says. "Practice your tricks."

Komarov comes in cleanly this time: "Golden Eagle, Control. Please be mindful of your words. Over."

"Yes, be mindful of your words." I push off with hands and feet, tuck into a spin. Flickering images: panels and lights and storage lockers, and Leonov with the camera.

"Very good," he says. "Nine-point-five from the Soviet judge. Now let's do it for real."

We are getting into position when the voice comes back: "Golden Eagle, our visual signal is still not great but it is time for the broadcast. We are transmitting across the country via the Lightning satellite system. Say something for the people. Over."

On the camera now, the red light is real. Millions of eyes. I freeze.

I become aware of Leonov's hand circling, a director's prompt.

I am just about to start talking when he speaks. "Greetings to the Soviet people, who have sent us on this glorious voyage. And to all the people of the world, whom we are proud to represent."

He stops. Does he want me to start?

Too late: he continues. "We are, in fact, speechless with pride, to be on this voyage to the moon. And excitement. As they say, we are head over heels."

An urgent index finger. This time I recognize my cue. But when I push into my spin, momentum and judgment are wrong, and as everything flashes by I inadvertently kick the camera.

A stabbing horror. What will they think?

I have tangled everything up into a weightless knot of limbs and camera and cord; Leonov pushes me away to secure the camera. "We have not rehearsed our camera work unfortunately. But it is only because we have been so busy practicing the flight itself, and everything we must do once we get to our destination. In fact, let's have a look." He moves the camera smoothly towards the starboard porthole. "The moon. We will of course not be the first to go into lunar orbit, but we may have a surprise for the world once we get there. And we are close. Already you can see how much larger and more three-dimensional it appears than the flat circle one sees from Earth."

I glance over at the porthole in my module, but the angle's wrong. I resist the urge to push into the descent module and have a look. I'll be seeing it soon enough.

"But of course…" (He pulls away from the porthole and pans smoothly over to the other side.) "…our drab destination is not as beautiful as you, dear Earth. Though far away, you are closer to our hearts than ever. We look forward to sharing the rest of this voyage with you, and to falling into your loving arms once it is over."

"Thank you all for sharing in this great triumph," I add.

Leonov glares back at me and turns the camera off. It's over now, thank God.

"That was not a nine-point-five," I admit.

"No, it was not."

"I wanted it to be perfect." As if wanting were enough. "We've had our share of accidents."

He retrieves his sketchpad and tray of charcoals from next to his form-fitted couch; I realize that, on top of everything else, we did not show him sketching in space. I am waiting for: what? Anger?

But he just nods. "We have indeed."

•••

In the window the moon has a clarity that takes my breath away.

I've seen it as a waxing crescent every twenty-eighth day of my life, weather permitting; the features are the same ones I've always known, their wonderful evocative names drilled into my head through months of training. On the sunlit side I can see the Sea of Crises and the Sea of Fertility; the terminator has brought morning to the innocent Sea of Serenity and the haunted Sea of Tranquility, and it's creeping westward to touch the place Leonov will be landing: the Ocean of Storms.

Of course, it all looks different. Not just round and real. New with the knowledge that we have a chosen place in its history, that—if all goes according to plan, and maybe if it

27

doesn't, everyone from now on will associate it with our names. Or his name, at least.

He is at my elbow now, looking, too. Sketchpad and charcoal still in hand. "It is a lot closer now, isn't it?"

"It is closer." Nothing to do but agree.

"What we've seen before was the earth's moon. Our image. You see it blue by day sometimes but that is an illusion. This is the real moon, Boris."

On the shadowed side there are still visible features, lit faintly blue by earthlight, brighter (it seems) than one would get from a full moon back home. It does look fantastic. "I suppose you want to sketch it."

"It would be nice. Before we have to reposition."

Silently I yield the porthole. Should I apologize for not giving him the chance to look like an artist on camera? No: surely this is enough.

He wedges himself back into place in the couch, with a clear view outside. His hand flies across the paper: circles and circles and circles. Still he speaks: "You have to wonder what's the best spot."

"The best spot?"

"We're landing in a flat easy place, close to the lunar equator. Which of course makes sense for a first landing. Still..." Still the hand sketches; still the eyes dart back and forth between paper and distant target. His ability to stay focused is, I must grudgingly admit, exceptional.

"What are the other options? Do you want to go to Tranquility?"

"Maybe not there. But one does get curious…"

"There's no way they'd send us. Not after what happened. Especially not on a first mission. Even the ones who are the least…superstitious…would be overruled by the ones who'd say, 'Why take chances?' They have their irrationalities, just like anyone. Just look at the Sea of Crises. That could be the best spot, on a purely selenographical basis…"

"It's not." His hand and eyes don't skip a beat.

"Still." I breathe to heal the sting of pedantic correction. "Hypothetically, it might be better, but what mission planner would opt for the Sea of Crises?"

"I'm sure the 'seas' aren't much different than the Ocean of Storms." On he sketches, relentless. It is, I must admit, a competent rendering, far better than I could do. "They're probably the lunar equivalent of the Kazakh steppe, not…Lake Baikal or the Lena Pillars. So I am curious what the best spot would be, in terms of sheer beauty. Not that I'll ever know…"

This is entirely too much. "Stop complaining."

"Who's complaining? I'm just observing."

"It sounds like you're complaining."

"Very well." Still he works, machine-like. "If you don't like my observations, I can keep them to myself."

"It will make for a quieter trip…"

This at last diverts his attention from the sketch: an ugly sideways look.

Time for an apology? No, I cannot. "I'm just observing."

Against his will he smiles a little. "I will keep my observations to myself. On the home trip, too. After you pick me up, I will tell you nothing about what it was like down there."

"If I even pick you up, after your trip down there." Perhaps that will put him in his place.

He grins. "You would be in more trouble than me."

"How do you figure?"

"I would fly around the moon a bit. Sightsee. Perhaps crash into it at the end. A quick painless way to go…"

Like Yuri, I don't say.

"…whereas you would come back to a living hell. Public inquiry, humiliation. Perhaps a trial and a place in the gulag. At the very least, endless questions."

"Nonsense. I will be the mournful hero. The noble crewmember who tried to save you but could not." I smile. We are joking, right? I think we are joking. Do we joke? "The last man to see you alive. The key to the mystery."

He laughs. "There will be no mystery, Boris! I will tell them everything. By radio."

"I'll sabotage your radio." Now we're talking absurdities; the lunar lander is buried under its shroud, and I'll never so much as see the inside; unlike on the ill-starred Apollo, there's no transfer tunnel. Leonov will have to spacewalk over to it once we're in lunar orbit; I don't even have a spacesuit.

"How? With your mind?"

I give a grim look of amusement, something far less than a smile. "Sometimes speaking things aloud makes them happen."

He resumes his sketch in silence. A quick separation movement with the thrusters.

I should apologize, but I do not.

Instead I push myself over to the other porthole. Earth is an amazing and intricate sculpture, the most detailed and beautiful work of art one could possibly imagine; I've seen it from up here before, but of course never from this far.

I unstow my camera and start taking pictures; I can do this, at least.

Again and again I look at the image in the viewfinder, the impossible image of a beautiful peaceful globe. A world that makes sense. Everyone I love is down there, and I am floating free, on a trip they would all envy, with a man I hate.

●●●

"Golden Eagle, Control. Are you ready to do some work up there? Over."

"Control, Golden Eagle." Leonov yells over the sanitary unit's vacuum noise. He has removed the cap and inserted his penis into the yellow cone and is busy, one presumes, urinating. "What do you need? Over."

31

"No talking while you piss," I mutter.

After a moment, the distant headset voice: "Golden Eagle, we are picking up some background noise. Over."

"One moment, Control." He finishes and squeezes himself out before turning off the device's vacuum.

"Golden Eagle, we need a realignment so we can prepare for the mid-course correction. Over."

"In a moment, Control. Taking care of urgent business."

"Make sure you wash your hands," I observe.

He gives me a dirty look as he quickly wipes down the device. Then he floats back into the descent module and starts strapping in. I can't help noticing that his hands themselves are still unwiped. "Control, Golden Eagle. I am getting settled in now..." He places his unwiped hands on the controllers; I shudder.

"Glad I have my own set of controllers." I float in after him and take my position in the right seat. "I'd hate to think I'm touching your penis secondhand."

A smirk. Then to ground: "...and we are aligning with the flight path. Over."

Thruster noise. A quick rotation about the yaw axis and we are back in proper position, more or less, although Control will still need to do a precise alignment with the sensors. Once again there is nothing outside but blackness and sun.

After the pause: "Golden Eagle, Control. Let us know when you are ready for Ground Control Mode. Over."

Leonov presses buttons on the Critical Command Panel to enable the groundlink. "Control, Golden Eagle. Ground Control enabled. Over."

Once our words find them, there are more thruster sounds. "Golden Eagle, we have acquired the sun with the 106-K sensors. Monitoring the 107-K now..."

Smaller pulses now from the thrusters. An automated process, unlike what we read about for the Apollo. It is possible for it to go wrong in the middle, to mistake the sun for the moon or vice versa; I wait for more thruster firings, noisy confirmation that the system is causing havoc. But it does in fact go smoothly. Or so it seems.

"...and the 100-K sensors are picking up the alignment stars. Please confirm through the sextant. You should have Epsilon Sagittarii at 8.2 up, 3.7 left."

Sagittarius. The archer. I smile; it shouldn't matter, but it does. "Control, give me a moment to get set up." I unbuckle, retrieve the porthole covers, and attach them. Then, to the sextant. I adjust the knobs and there it is. "Epsilon Sagittari is at 8.2 up, 2.3 left. Over."

"Golden Eagle, Control. We will fire the Block-D for two seconds in the posigrade direction. Ten meters per second correction. Roll 3-7, Pitch 1-2, Yaw 0-5. Over."

It takes effort not to turn on the rendezvous screen to confirm that we are, in fact, pointed at the moon.

"Hold one, Control." I strap back in and we both read the numbers on the console. All the computation has been done on the ground; we have nothing to do but alert them if the

Block-D doesn't fire, and cut it off manually if it goes on too long.

And trust. The hardest part.

Leonov butts in. "Go ahead, Control."

"Golden Eagle, engine will fire at Moscow Time nineteen hours, one minute, twenty-three seconds. Over."

"Very well, Control." My hand hovers over the cutoff. I raise my other arm to look at my watch.

On cue the machine starts, a brief calculated bump in the back, one, two, and my hand mashes the cutoff button but already the rocket has stopped, it is perfect.

"It's fine," Leonov says. "A triumph of central planning."

"A triumph." I smile; we are indeed in this together and it does feel perfect; we are headed straight like an arrow towards the invisible spot just ahead of the moon where its gravity will send us arcing around its backside and into position to fire our engines again and settle into lunar orbit.

Still I turn on the rendezvous screen, just to make sure.

Leonov laughs. "It's too late for that now!" He restarts the rotation, unbuckles, pushes himself into the orbital module, removes the porthole covers. "Everything in its proper time. And now it's time to dump our piss."

"All right. Time to dump our piss." Something we can't do right before course correction, for fear of obstructing our view of the stars. But it's something we both love watching.

The spacecraft spins slowly, the blinding sunlight sweeping through the orbital module. I position myself; he activates the valve and joins me. We watch the droplets spew forth, golden and glorious in the sunlight; they freeze and start sublimating. An indescribable view, impossible for him to sketch, I'm sure.

"It is nice to take a piss wherever you want," Leonov says.

"You're not pissing. The spacecraft is pissing."

"Well...down there, I'll piss wherever I want."

"Only because you'll be wearing a diaper."

• • •

In the absence of anything else to look at I have drifted back into the descent module; his sketchpad's cardboard back is tucked into a tension pocket, with the pictures fanned out. I can just see the edge of the moon sketch...

"You can take it out and look at it," he calls from the orbital module. "Just be careful not to smudge the charcoal."

I am annoyed that he can read my desires; there is no room for secrets in here. But I do take it out, and he has indeed made an accurate rendering of the moon. "Do you think it's cursed?"

"Don't be superstitious."

"I watched the recording of the Apollo 8 crew."

"The Christmas broadcast?"

"Yes, the one where they read from Genesis." The last normal transmission.

"It was a lovely bit of television."

"It seemed so at the time, yes." 1968. America's cursed year. (Not that the ones on either side were much better.) "Our broadcast probably didn't look as good."

"No matter. They got the television right. But the missions..." A head shake. "For us, it will be the other way around."

"I hope so." A bittersweet thought. Would we be here if the Apollo missions had gone normally? Probably not. But of course, after the triumphant broadcast came the explosion. Damage to the spacecraft, one oxygen tank gone and the other leaking fast, carbon dioxide rising...

"You never listened to the other recordings, did you?"

"No."

"That's good. No need for that."

"Indeed." Imagining it is bad enough. "They were foolish to press on with the program."

"They had identified the issue. The maintenance logs. The damage to the tank. I think there was a heater that had been built to the wrong specifications."

The eternal debate. "They were foolish to press on. Just to meet some arbitrary deadline. What did it get them? A year later, another disaster."

"Apollo 10." He shakes his head.

I look back at the drawing: the Sea of Tranquility, a perfect name for the solar system's largest cemetery. Stafford and Cernan resting forever. Another bittersweet feeling, another failure that allowed us to be here.

"It's not cursed." He nods at the drawing. "It's waiting for us."

"We've had accidents, too." Near the edge of the hand-drawn moon a crumb of charcoal clings to the paper, despite the lack of gravity. I blow on it, but it's still there. I touch it and: a smudge, crossing the bright arc of the sunlit side.

"You!" His face: pure exasperation. "It's…"

Embarrassment stabs me, direct and brutal, face and chest.

He takes the sketchpad away. "The charcoals smudge easily."

"You should have cleaned it up better. Or…rolled it up, maybe."

"I wanted to touch it up tonight before bed." He works his finger over the moon side of the smudge: a new dark sea.

"I don't remember that feature." Even I know it's a poor attempt at humor.

"Is it too much to apologize, Boris?"

A long breath. Trying to equalize. "I am sorry. I really am."

"It's…" He produces his charcoals again, adds some white highlights, takes the black and sharpens the arc between sunlit moon and infinite space. "It's not what it was. But maybe I can clean it up." A pause, a gaze. Is it my imagination, or is he looking at the Sea of Tranquility? Thinking again of those who did not come back.

"I'm glad we're not landing there." An accident I had nothing to do with, at least.

"There is an attitude in Japanese art about embracing mistakes, embracing limitations." Leonov hovers over the line between light and dark, work and contemplation. "How everything is impermanent. Unfinished. Imperfect."

"Not a useful attitude in our line of work." Unspoken: all the deaths, on both sides. More American than Soviet, but starting with Bondarenko and ending, of course, with Bykovsky and Makarov.

"Indeed. But here we are."

I float into the orbital module and place the covers back on the portholes so we can be oblivious to our journey. Then I retrieve my sleeping bag. Unfurled, it floats like a giant blue ghost; I attach it over the hatch through which Leonov will egress in two days on his way to the surface of the moon. The last time I'll see him? Through the interior hatch I glimpse him strapped back in, sketchpad on a fresh page; I imagine him asking Control for permission to reorient the massive spacecraft stack. Staying up late and burning more propellant, just to produce a new perfect work of art.

●●●

In the morning after a night of unremembered dreams I am awakened by radio noises.

It is the day of our arrival at the moon. Only three missions have flown here before: the two ill-fated Apollos, and sandwiched between them, our circumlunar flight.

As Leonov chats with Control I retrieve the toilet device. I am in a morning state of arousal common to most men, so it is somewhat awkward to position the contraption.

"...we are both well-rested and...uhh...eager to start the day," my commander is saying. "Fuel cells steady and pressure gauges look good. Over."

The pause in their response is even more noticeable than it was; the speed of light is indeed finite. "Very well, Golden Eagle. Your trajectory is nominal. We are running computations on the BESM-6 and will radio up lunar orbit insertion commands in one hour. Over."

I am finally completely inserted in the receptacle when it occurs to me that, if I turn on the vacuum switch, it will tip them off as to what I'm doing. So I hold off. Leonov gives me a funny look before finally turning back to his business. "Control, how did everyone enjoy last night's broadcast? Over."

"Golden Eagle, we couldn't fix the issues with the television reception. But the country is excited. The world is excited. They are eager to see a successful mission. Over."

"We'll be sure to take plenty of pictures." Leonov glares at me. "Golden Eagle out."

I turn on the vacuum. "Finally." But the interior valves are taking their time. Pressures are building. Then at last: the flow. Blessed relief: I moan.

"No using the vacuum hose for lewd purposes," Leonov says. "Whether or not your wife's putting out, that's none of my business. I only ask that you don't use the spacecraft as a substitute."

"Very funny." I've never been one for talking while urinating, so I pinch off the conversation, rather than myself. Then I make a big show of cleaning the device, and my hands.

"They must not have seen much on the ground," he says. "The broadcast."

"I'm sure they saw enough. You'll have a chance to show them a lot more soon."

"As long as we fix the reception."

Done with the device, I pull myself into the interior hatchway. "Well, you'll have the television, you'll have the camera. And if that's not enough, you can draw them a picture."

"Indeed. By the way, what did you dream about?"

"I don't remember. Why do you ask?"

"I was up late. It looked like you were dreaming."

I pull myself into the descent module, settle in to my sculpted couch. On the other side I catch a glimpse of his sketchpad, tucked in to a different spot. "Up late drawing?"

"I did, for a bit," he admits. "I still got a good night's sleep."

His tone seems overly friendly; he's a different person than he was yesterday, a phenomenon I've noticed more than once in training. It's more off-putting than constant tension, although on days like today it makes me wonder if I judge him too harshly. "What's your birthday, by the way?"

"What does that have to do with anything?"

"I'm just curious. I never remember it."

"May 30th."

"That figures." A Gemini. It does explain many things: a twin, never the same person from one situation to the next. And always looking for his other half. Perhaps that's what he had with Yuri.

"What figures?"

"Nothing." I scan gauges and indicator lights. Purposelessly, for he's already done the morning checklists.

"I had quite the dream myself."

It does seem like people only ask you about your dreams when they're eager to share theirs. Still, no way to avoid it now. "Tell me about your dream."

"It was very vivid. I landed on the moon, and Tom Stafford was there. He had survived the crash, but he had no radio. He'd just been…living there, these past few months."

"That must have been terrifying."

"It wasn't scary! It felt very natural. I caught a glimpse of him through the front window on descent and somehow all I thought was: *Oh, there he is. I'm sure he'll want to talk to me.* And I landed, and he was just standing there. Watching. And I got out, and we shook hands, and he said, 'I've been waiting for you.' When I woke up it took me a moment to realize it hadn't happened."

"Was the other one there?"

"Cernan? No, I didn't see him."

"What happened to him?"

"I don't know. Stafford never said."

"How did you talk? On the radio?"

"I don't know. I just remember what he said: 'I've been waiting for you.'"

"In Russian, or English?"

"Boris!" Leonov laughs. "There is no logic in dreams."

"Nothing that can survive the morning, at least." Nothing on the gauges looks particularly abnormal. Although...is that maneuvering fuel reading what it was? Did he really reposition the spacecraft, just to make another sketch? I'm racking my brain, trying to remember the number from last night. Perhaps Control has it logged...

"Let's have breakfast, shall we?" He floats out of his seat and I'm treated—or perhaps subjected is a better word—to a view of his ass in the hatch. Meanwhile I remove the covers from the descent module portholes and steal a glimpse at the sketchpad; it does indeed look like he's drawn another picture.

"What did you sketch? When you stayed up late?"

"The moon. What else?" In the orbital module he removes the other window covers, then retrieves two packages of porridge and starts injecting hot water.

I float on up to join him. "From sight, or memory?"

"I repositioned the whole spacecraft stack, to draw it once more from sight. I burned up precious maneuvering fuel just to have a better sketch. It may make rendezvous different after the landing, but that's a sacrifice I'm willing to make for my art." He laughs.

"I just…need to know."

"Boris, what do you take me for?"

"It seems like a reasonable question."

"If you're an unreasonable person. The things you worry about…"

"All right."

"I mean…what do you take me for?"

"All right! Enough. I'm sorry I brought it up."

He hands me my porridge. "Do you want to see the sketch, at least?"

Does my response matter? Clearly he's eager to show it. "Sure, why not?"

Leaving his breakfast in midair, he floats back down to retrieve the sketchpad. I eat; the food would be miserable if I weren't so hungry. Back he comes, art in hand. "I took a little more care, brushing it off. I'll still have to coat it when we get back, but it should keep until then."

He hands me the sketchpad. This I did not expect. I place my food in empty space and gingerly grab the back cardboard; the pages fan upward in the weightless air and I wipe my fingers on my jumpsuit before pressing everything back together and eyeing the new drawing: earthglow shadow, dark lunar seas, starburst crater rays, and the bright arc where nothingness begins. "That's very nice. Better than the other one. Even before the accident."

"Thank you!"

From the warmth of his response I feel I've messed up, by paying him a compliment. "Are you going to tell them it's a copy?"

"A copy?"

"Well, if you weren't looking at the moon as you did it, I assume you were looking at the other picture."

"Boris."

I leave the sketchpad floating, retrieve my porridge. "I guess you can tell them what you want."

"We both can." He grins. "But I repositioned the spacecraft stack, to draw it from sight."

Even now I have no idea whether he is joking.

I put water into a powdered juice packet, shake it to mix it. "So what was it like down there, anyway?"

"Down there?"

"In your dream. On the moon."

"I told you I wouldn't tell you."

I laugh. "That's after the real trip! This doesn't count."

"It was like a dirty beach. A dirty beach under a black sunny sky." A sip of juice, then he returns to his porridge.

And I am turning back to the window, the one away from the sun, all the featureless blackness of cosmic space. Thinking of childhood, the father I never knew, the mother who was my everything even though she was constantly gone. Working hard at the clinic, or disappearing into other rooms to talk to the adults. Whispered conversations about ghettos and ravines in the Ukraine, Slavs with grudges and Germans with machine guns, working together despite the war, just for this one thing. And that word, the first time I heard it: Jew. I remember asking her: *What is a Jew?* And her answer: *Us. We are Jews.*

I could not understand. I still cannot understand, but especially then I could not understand. All the things she didn't want a young boy to know about, for his own sake. All the things that would have been happening to us, if we lived where most Jews lived.

•••

Our velocity is increasing.

It was at its highest when we were leaving Earth orbit; it fell steadily as we climbed and our planet tried to pull us home. At some point in the night it was down around a thousand meters per second. Since then it's been picking back up, like an amusement park ride cresting a hill; we're falling into the moon's domain.

Today's main business is simple, but substantial: to make sure we stay there.

"Golden Eagle, Contr..." (A burst of static obscures Beregovoy's voice.) "...eters for your Block-D..." (More static.) "...er."

Leonov and I trade uneasy glances. We are in this together, for a little while, at least. "Control, Golden Eagle. Please repeat transmission. Over."

"Golden Eagle, Control. We have..." (Crackle. More crackle.) "...ck-D firing. Over."

There are times each day where our words are relayed by radio ships as the world turns, but we should have line-of-sight right now. And we need this transmission desperately. Our Block-D must fire while we are out of radio contact, as we are passing behind the moon; we need to do that to enter lunar orbit. Control controls many things, but not the laws of simple geometry; they have to finish programming our spacecraft before we pass over the lunar horizon. And we need to know the parameters, for we'll be monitoring it alone.

"Control, Golden Eagle. Transmission quality is poor. Standing by for Block-D parameters. Over."

If they cannot program the burn it is not, as they say, the end of the world. But it will be the end of the moon. The end of our dreams for landing. Or, perhaps, the end of Leonov's dreams; we will swing around the far side, whipped by lunar gravity, and head home early. Of course, if our failure is his fault, and Kamanin is looking for someone to command the next mission...someone with experience...

Dark territory for my thoughts to overfly. Despite all my issues with Korolev's golden boy, I do not wish to linger here. I place my hands on my headset, eager to catch the transmission through sheer force of concentration, willpower making up for lack of radio power.

"Golden Eag..." (Static.) "...ck-D parameters as follows. Retrograde firing of the..." (More static. It lasts forever.)

Leonov and I share another glance, speak in the secret language of crewmembers who know one another's complaints but are too professional to speak them aloud and step on the transmission. *Retrograde firing of the Block-D stage...the one part we already know.* Posigrade would simply send us home earlier.

"Control, Golden Eagle," I transmit. "Say again all after 'posigrade firing,' over."

After the delay: "Retrograde, Golden Eagle!" Beregovoy's alarm is apparent; my face floods with feeling as I realize my error. "Retrograde firing of the Block-D. Firing will be Moscow Time one..." (Another long crackle, and the rest of the transmission is lost.)

"Control, Golden Eagle." If Leonov is losing patience, I can't tell; all gauges are normal. "Say again all after 'Moscow Time,' over."

The words make their way. Then: "Golden Eagle, Control. Retrograde firing of the Block-D. Moscow Time one-zero..." (Static.)

Another shared look: *Beregovoy is repeating the parts we already know. What other rocket stage would we fire? The old man's going senile.* If these shared moments keep adding up, Leonov and I are going to become friends, very much against my will.

"Control, Golden Eagle. We have the firing direction. Say again all after Moscow Time one-zero. Over."

"Golden Eagle, Moscow Time one-zero-one hours and..." (Static.)

We do not have forever for this. We do not even have all day. But we have a few hours, and no more important task on the agenda than to copy the most important information of our lives, one number at a time.

•••

When at last the work is done, we can finally see the moon.

It is large now; it is close enough we do not need to reorient to see it. It has swollen to fill the porthole; it is solid and real and *here*, a massive giant sphere. We are approaching the shadowed side and so we're headed for a solar eclipse, the most total of our lives. The bright side is a narrow scythe; the blinding sun just beyond, heading for oblivion.

In a few short moments it is gone. Rays of light beyond the edge, fabulous lighting for a few transient moments. And on the dim earthward side, mountains and craters and harsh features lit faintly blue by our home planet's glow.

"It's hard to believe this is the same moon we've been seeing all our lives," Leonov says.

The earthglow ends in a clear firm arc. Beyond it, a black void. A hole in the stars. And there *are* stars now, an impossible infinity, a supreme array of unblinking light, with slight but innumerable variances in brightness and size and whiteness, ranging from cold electric blues to old orange warmth, summoning feelings inverse to their actual temperatures.

My eyes return to the vast moonscape, a cool dark dream. "I've always wanted to go. Even when I was a child, and it was just a...distant circle. I remember thinking: how sunny it must be. How peaceful." How many images can my mind hold? How long can I hold on to them? "Can you imagine what it looks like down there right now? I mean...there are snowy nights in the country under a full moon where the light is like this, and you want to fly above. But here, looking down..." The rest goes unsaid.

"Indeed." Leonov pulls out the Zenith, snaps a few pictures. End of the roll: he rewinds the film.

"No sketchpad?"

"It's changing too fast. I'm sure I can draw it from memory later. Or pictures. Although in this low light..." He leaves the camera floating; he edges closer to the porthole, taking more than his share of space, and I'm reminded why I sometimes catch myself hating him. I'm just about to put it into words when he pushes himself back. "Actually, I'll go watch from the orbital module."

I occupy the space he vacates. "Do you think we'll be back?"

"Of course! I'm sure of it." Again, his ass in the hatch, his puffy weightless face a small sliver beyond, too distant to be reassuring. He won't be back, so he doesn't care.

"I mean, getting past all the propaganda about…building a Bolshevik utopia, drawing a new perfect society on a blank page. Realistically…for us…how many more times?"

"They say three or four, at least." The party line. He knows I know it, too.

"Always those words. 'They say…' Like a glove, to keep your hands from getting dirty. To keep from leaving fingerprints at the scene of the crime…"

"I'm not in charge of these things, Boris! I'm no more in control than you are."

"Still…they say a lot of things. But we know how they get. When there's money to be spent, and no more accomplishments to be made."

"Well you would know, that's for sure." A rare acknowledgment from him of my struggles.

"Do you think I have a shot? If they do three or four more?"

"You want to go down there too?"

"Doesn't everyone?"

"Obviously it will depend on a lot of things. We've got a lot to do on this mission, before anyone has those discussions."

"But you could put in a word with Kamanin, when it's all over. I'm sure that would mean something."

"We've got a lot to do on this mission. Before anyone has those discussions." He's forming his own party line. "Let's enjoy this mission in the meantime. We're here now. Nothing else is guaranteed."

I'm not sure what's worse: the fact that he's right, or the fact that he's right. But there is no point pressing the issue. So: back to the porthole, the sweeping view. Mine alone. The moon is larger now; across the airless distance, the earthlit portion seems close enough to touch. Beyond, the black void is growing.

• • •

Without discussing the matter we fall back into the loving arms of our custom-fitted couches. One with our spacecraft, so one with each other, like it or not.

"Golden Eagle, Control. Five minutes until we lose signal. Your trajectory is within normal limits. The firing has been programmed. You can reposition manually if you'd like. Over."

They have done all they can for us, for now. Surely it is hard for them to accept: after all this hard work there are no more action items, except to wait in silence.

"Control, Golden Eagle. We are repositioning. Over." Leonov pulses the thrusters; the spacecraft stack swings around, twenty meters of metal turning slowly in space. I scan the instruments for evidence he's done something wrong. But everything is as expected. And now we are flying backwards, facing Earth but unable to see it beyond the walls of our spacecraft as it dips towards the lunar horizon.

"Golden Eagle, Control. Three minutes until signal loss. Alignment is good. Over."

"Copy, Control." We can see the alignment as well as they can. But perhaps they're trying to reassure us before we slip into the dark. Perhaps they're trying to reassure themselves.

I could turn on the rendezvous camera. Try to catch a last glimpse of Earth…

No. Instead: another scan of the panel. The kerosene and liquid oxygen pressures in the Block-D are as expected; all the indicator lights and needles are smooth and steady and reassuring, as much as anything can be in the middle of such an endeavor. I feel like a child, making sure the door is open and the hallway light is on, then staring at it for reassurance as I wait for my dreams.

"Golden Eagle, Control. Less than a minute remaining. We'll talk to you soon." And then, as if they distrust the certainty embedded in that statement: "Good luck. Over."

Outside, darkness and stars. So many things have gone wrong on my way here. And yet, here I am.

"Good luck yourself," Leonov says, and there is no way to know if they heard.

If the alignment is wrong we will, at best, be headed home early. At worst we'll be in a bad orbit, unable to accomplish our mission, lost in space. So I keep checking the alignment. But the alignment is correct.

Minutes pass in silence. The darkness is complete in the half of the sky that's been eclipsed by the moon. The stars are impressive but impassive. I am quite all right with the fact that we're not talking.

Then: sunlight at the edges of the portholes. No more stars. And: a bright arc of crater-mottled light, coming beneath us from behind like a slow-moving wave. Sunrise.

On the other side, more craters, and mountains, a rough and rugged scene. Alien.

"The far side," Leonov says simply.

"One minute to firing." As if to remind him.

Again the emptiness. I am glad we are not talking. We'll do what we have to do. That is enough.

When the timer is done the Block-D fires, pushing against the mass of metal, pushing against us. After these weightless days the gentle pressure feels like violence. I lift my hand towards the panel. If the firing goes on too long we will crash into the moon in a half-orbit, or sooner: another one-way trip for two hapless humans.

But the firing is correct.

Now we can unstrap; now we can go to our separate portholes and watch the lunar landscape, sharp in the airless sunlight, unreal. Imagining the violence that formed this:

moonquakes, volcanoes, meteors. All the fury that forged this desolate peace.

"Ten minutes until we pick up signal," Leonov says.

"It will be nice to talk to someone."

He says nothing. And I am quite all right with that.

• • •

"...olden Eagle, Control." Their voices, right on time. "Come in. Over."

"Control, Golden Eagle." I can't think of much to say. We're still here. Isn't that enough? "Everything has gone according to plan. Over."

This of course they know already. Their delayed acknowledgment: "If it hadn't, Golden Eagle, we'd have been talking already. Over."

"Unless we kept our mouths shut," Leonov mutters.

"Golden Eagle, we are monitoring your orbit and passing parameters to the BESM-6." Gone are the earlier issues, all the staticky transmissions just ghostly memories now. No explanation. "We will pass up circularization parameters soon. Have you taken lunch yet, over?"

"We have not," Leonov says.

We are not waiting for their permission, but a few seconds later they give it anyway. "Take your lunch, Golden Eagle. We'll talk to you soon. Over.

Wordlessly we take our tubes of borscht. Leonov stays in the orbital module to look out "his" porthole while I pull myself back into the descent module to watch through "mine." I recognize now what a clever move it was for him to "give" me this window while we were approaching the moon. Short-sightedness on my part: had I gone in there first, I would have a roomier space now to eat and observe.

We settle in. The low spot in our orbit is on the far side, where we fired the Block-D; as we climb to apolune the view is broad, a vast sun-blasted panorama, harsh and bleak. There is more color than expected, but not much: a bleached desert tan. I imagine white bones baking under black sky, although: no. The flesh on the bones, there would be nothing to make it decay. So: meat, desiccated in the relentless heat. Then again, no living thing would ever be unsuited down there. Although, perhaps, from the force of a crash...

Positive thoughts, positive thoughts. My wife is always telling me, I must think positive thoughts. We are here; we will redefine what it means to go to the moon. Now: two deaths. A hundred years from now: how many lives? A new worker's paradise in this empty place. Blocky five-story apartment buildings of lunar concrete, a room for every member of the family. Workers riding moon busses to mining sites under the black sky...I can see them waiting in their moon suits, a lunch pail in every hand. Children playing outside, throwing moon dust like snowballs. Although the footprints would accumulate forever...no wind or rain to wipe the slate clean...

As I suck on my borscht I catch myself peeking through the interior hatch, watching Leonov watch the moon. Is he thinking about these things—the short history, the endless possibility? Or just what he has to do? His face betrays no clue.

Below, the shadows are lengthening as we head towards the terminator. The landscape, more gray. Our orbit is taking us over two seas: the northern edge of Fertility, full of empty promise; the southern shore of Tranquility, awash in its sad past. Then: craters in bright highlands. And at last, the Ocean of Storms, down there at the edge of shadow, waiting to be known, tomorrow.

•••

By the time our tubes are empty it is dark down below; we are still sunlit, but it will be over soon enough.

I worry about the communications issues recurring, but the transmissions remain clear. Control sends the circularization parameters and we copy them as darkness abruptly overtakes us outside.

On the surface of the moon: earthglow again, the dreamy desert night.

Again we settle into the couches, strap in. Again we lose radio contact with Earth, exactly on schedule. We read our lines, playing our roles: no audience but our egos. Again everything happens to perfection, smoother than any simulation.

I scan the instrumentation in disbelief: all the illuminated buttons in memorized patterns; the indicator needles hovering where needed, as if by magic. It goes against my whole spaceflight career that nothing has gone wrong so far; I am the Apollo program of cosmonauts. But nothing has gone wrong so far.

Then again, I felt this way on Union-2, before the problems. Perhaps the bad luck is massing its forces, waiting to attack in one overwhelming surge. Perhaps it's only a matter of time...

Positive thoughts, positive thoughts. Leonov—Blondie—he is my opposite, in that way as in others.

We unstrap again, look down once more at the sunlit far side. As if reading my mind he says: "Better than you expected, huh?"

"I must admit, I am a little surprised."

"Given the career you've had, I don't blame you." Another acknowledgment of my past: the lean years waiting to launch, and afterwards, almost worse, the fat years that are somehow making me hungrier. I am surprised that he's been paying attention, that he cares; as he floats back up into the orbital module he clasps me on the shoulder with real warmth. "It's all right, though. You're with me now."

Korolev was my enemy, and he was close with Korolev. But perhaps he's not my enemy.

Far below, rugged terrain: bright sharp craters overlaid over other old ones. No erosion down there, so: worn only by time and gravity, and the haphazard micrometeorite rain. Circles within circles, circles overlapping circles, circles next to circles: arranged in lines, in patterns, in strange designs. All similar, none the same. Circles and circles and circles.

I glance up: he is also at his window, enraptured by the pitted moonscape. Or, perhaps, the mission. "As smooth as a peeled egg."

"We'll be coming up on earthrise soon." The famous photograph, from our circumlunar flight: the one that wowed the world.

"Get out the camera. You can snap a few pictures."

An unexpected blessing. Again the thought: Will he be the same tomorrow? Nothing is guaranteed. "You don't want to take them?"

He smiles. "I learned long ago: never copy another artist's work. People will think you're jealous."

I unstow the camera, position myself by the porthole.

"I did try, as a child," he adds. "Tracing pictures of airplanes, pictures of landscapes. It's never satisfying if it isn't yours, if it isn't something new that you alone have brought to fruition."

A bright blue bulge on the horizon now, a mottled beautiful marble, shyly coming out of hiding. "It is quite a view." I take several pictures; perhaps I'll capture something new.

Leonov is watching, too. A tourist for now, enjoying the sights. "It does matter, who comes…"

The radio voice intrudes. Somehow unexpected, this interruption. "Golden Eagle, this is Control. Come in, over."

"Control, this is Golden Eagle." Leonov's voice spikes, annoyed. "Stand by for a minute, over." If I talked to them like that, I'd be grounded for life. He switches to intercom. "As I was saying, it does matter who comes first. People do judge these things. Are you original, or derivative? People mass-produce prints, make signed and numbered limited editions. Especially in the West. And I don't blame them. But anywhere you go, the original is worth more." His eyes find mine. "I'll sketch it later tonight, I'm sure. And tomorrow on the surface...I'll take some original photos." A massive grin: he is sure this is going to happen.

I'm starting to believe it too. But still: "You're not going to bring your sketchpad down there? Knock out a drawing or two on the surface of the moon? Then later on, you can say you did three or four..."

He laughs. "Don't sabotage things, Boris." On goes the radio. "Go ahead, Control."

The pause. Then: "Golden Eagle, your orbital parameters are as follows: apolune, one-five-zero-point-five kilometers, perilune, one-five-zero-point-one kilometers. You are looking good!" Cheers from the control room, chills down my spine: this is real. They are cheering for *us*. "I'm sure you've taken some pictures already. We'll have you shoot from the target list this orbit. Over."

"Thank you, Control. Golden Eagle out," Leonov says. Then to me: "Do you want to handle that?"

"You're letting me do something else?" An actual mission task. After the grief I gave him, this is a surprise.

"Who knows? These might be places you go."

So he will put in a word with Kamanin. My heart unclenches. "I thought nothing was guaranteed, after tomorrow."

"Nothing is guaranteed." A long, suspenseful pause. "But I could put in a word." Another communications delay. "Assuming you pick me up after I lift off from the surface."

Against my will, a smile cracks my mask. "You don't need to give me added incentive!"

He grins. "After that conversation we had…"

"Fair enough." My smile twists but widens. "It's a bargain, as they say."

I unstow the camera and float into the orbital module.

"Looks like the edge of Fertility." Leonov's porthole is orthogonal to mine, but we can still see some of the same landmarks. "I can see Langrenus down south."

"All right." I watch the moon scroll by. Down in the lunar sea there are individual craters without others around, solitary and beautiful. I hold off on photographing them: there will be time later.

Our first target is not, in fact, a place we're hoping to go, but something to avoid: the crash site. Nixon's famous statement: *Fate has ordained that the men who went to the moon to explore in peace will stay on the moon to rest in peace.* I shudder. Imagine instead: life. Apartment complexes, Khrushchev's slums, although they'll be calling them something else by then.

Still there is the thought: Leonov's dream. As the dark peaceful lowlands roll by and Fertility gives way to Tranquility, I raise the weightless camera. Imagine Stafford down there, eating God knows what, sitting patiently in the sunlit dust, watching the bright speck of our spacecraft as it streaks across the black sky. Waiting. Or maybe starting to walk west...

Is he thinking about it too? Leonov—Blondie. God help me, I'm starting to see it his way.

•••

The rest of the afternoon passes simply: more photography, bathroom breaks, talks with Control—Beregovoy and then Komarov, after the shift change—about telemetry and data, what gauges to keep an eye on, what modifications to make to the checklists. Soon the view outside isn't even a distraction; our portholes are like the ignored windows of a transport when you're halfway through a familiar flight. The moon has become routine.

I start heating dinner packets with the passion of a mechanic.

"Never thought it would seem normal, did you?" Leonov floats up, again reading my mind.

"You spend so many years wondering if it's going to happen...you see so many things go wrong..."

"Your career." Is there exasperation now in the words? Less warmth, at any rate. "Well, as I've said, you're with m..."

"It's not just about me! Our program! They were so...desperate for another triumph. I mean, Sunrise-2, the chances they were taking..." His spacewalk had in fact been a risky affair; it is tough to tell whether his stories grew more harrowing because he was stretching the truth, or coming to terms with how close he'd come to being trapped outside. Maybe after Yuri's crash...

"You would have flown Sunrise-2, too. If they'd let you. You would have trained up and gone outside. Who knows? Maybe it wouldn't have ended well."

A flush of anger. The chicken feels like a child's fevered forehead; I hand him his packet.

He is monitoring my temperature gauges; he can see he pushed it. "I shouldn't say that. Who knows what would have happened. It might have gone well." A flatness: Is he saying this because he believes it, or because he has to? "Still. We were taking chances. All of us. You would have flown East-5. You would have flown Sunrise-3, and Sunrise-2, and Sunrise-1, if they'd picked you."

"That's beside the point." I should start eating. But: "Everyone could tell, things were starting to feel different. Gemini...by the time it wrapped up, they were ahead. Everyone could tell."

"And look where it got them. They tripped, they were so eager; they lost focus and tripped. Even harder than they would have tripped otherwise." Behind the façade I can see other thoughts organizing. "I will say...Korolev. When he went into the hospital..."

"Korolev." I pick at my bland tepid chicken. "You and I had a very different relationship with Korolev."

"We wouldn't be here, if it wasn't for him. *You* wouldn't be here."

"You and I had a very different relationship with him. You were chosen. Whereas if I was chosen, it was..." A rueful head shake; I glance out at the moon, cold and distant. "I know, intellectually I know, he got us most of the way here. I'm glad he made it out of the hospital, I'm glad he got to pick his successor. If Mishin had been in charge after-wards..."

A slow nod of contemplation. "Mishin is no leader. We never would have gotten here under Mishin. When Korolev was gone, Mishin started spinning through...paranoid, absurd scenarios for the landing. Landing a second Lunar Craft as backup, in case the first was damaged on landing. Landing a Moonwalker in case the cosmonaut needed to drive to the second craft..."

"Indeed. But Korolev..." Again, picking at the chicken. "Let's just say, he felt like an enemy. I was not glad when he died. But that was the day I knew I'd finally fly."

"Korolev was not your enemy. He liked you more than you realize."

"After he died, that's when I made it up here."

A slow nod from the golden boy. "Everyone makes mistakes, you know."

A bitter chuckle, remembering our talk: Japanese art and a smear of charcoal. "Is that where we're at now? Embracing imperfection?"

And here he is silent. For a long time he looks at the empty moon. Then: "My father was in the camps, you know."

"I did not know that."

"They don't encourage such talk. Around the office." A pinched smile. "But it was quite a time for mistakes. Leaders making up stories about...sabotage...to distract from their own failings. Conspiracy theories where the evidence of the plot never quite materialized, where the denunciations always served some other convenient purpose. Removing a romantic rival. Advancing oneself professionally. Korolev was caught too, you know; he knew what it was like to have enemies. The things that man endured..." He gives me a long slow look, as if knowing Korolev was a victim will make me forget my victimhood at Korolev's hands. "But it all started with absurdities. Knowing what he became, it is easy to forget what he and the others were, back in the thirties. Hungry dreamers, starving in cellars so they could launch us to utopia. Capabilities that were multiple orders of magnitude below what was required. And when the future didn't happen fast enough..." A shake of the head. "It was absurd, the factions that developed. Solid fuel versus liquid, this became a political argument. And among liquid fuels: Bolshevik liquid oxygen versus Trotskyite nitric acid. All because our so-called leaders believed lack of progress meant sabotage. Because they would rather believe everyone was against them, than accept they were humans, with flaws."

I take a deep breath. Trying to read his gauges. Or mine.

He continues: "As for my...other father, he was in the camps because another man, a Tatar..." (He says the ethnicity as if it's a slur.) "...slaughtered his horse. And my father, quite naturally, swore vengeance. So this...Tatar...rather than dealing with the situation directly, he made up a story about my father supposedly...sabotaging the harvest." (Decades of hidden bitterness.) "So my father was taken away to the camps. Our neighbors were encouraged to come and steal our food. Our family had to leave our village."

Again: "I did not know that." What else can you say, when you learn of someone's suffering? "I'm sorry, Alexei."

"But you know what? My father came back. They did eventually grant him a trial. The Tatar had to give up his position as head of the collective. And then...the war. We lost so many. But my family ended up moving to Kaliningrad when it was all over. All those beautiful buildings that used to be German. Those buildings were now ours! So even after all that had happened before—after everything that had happened to my own family!—I still supported Stalin. 'You should not malign the system because of the wrongdoings of a few individuals,' my father used to say whenever he heard criticism. We figured it was the Tatar's fault. The fault of...Yagoda, and the...others in the NKVD. So I still supported Stalin, even after all those...mistakes."

"You were...what, a teenager?"

"Old enough to know better. I even mourned when Stalin died! It was years before I burned the black armband I wore to mourn his death. So yes, people make mistakes. And what's worse, they hold on to them! They embrace them! Because to let go is to admit you were wrong. That you're human. And that's too much for most people."

"Well we won't need to worry about embracing our mistakes tomorrow." I smile. "Because we won't make any."

"Ha! Indeed. It will be as smooth as a peeled egg."

Again, a look out at the moon. It is starting to feel like a friend.

• • •

After dinner I am heading into the descent module when I run into Blondie floating back the other way, pen in hand; we collide.

"Your sketchpad's back in there." He had already removed his pen cap, of course, so there's damage from the run-in; I look forlornly at the ink slash on the chest of my jumpsuit; halfheartedly I scratch at it. "Even if it wasn't, I'm not your signed original." I lick spittle onto my finger, dab at the pen mark.

"Very funny." He isn't laughing. "I'm getting my cuff checklist. We've got work to do."

It will indeed be a long day for him tomorrow: putting on the Falcon spacesuit right after breakfast, spacewalking along the railing to the Lunar Craft. Separating and starting the descent (still fully clad in the spacesuit), touching down safely (God willing), popping out the side hatch, heading down the ladder, walking around. Two hours outside: planting the flag, collecting rock samples, deploying scientific experiments, taking photographs. And then: back in, *finally* repressurizing the craft (for it will have been unpressurized this whole time, to save on consumables) and removing his helmet faceplate, *finally* eating again—dinner, by this time—before lifting off at last to rendezvous with me. And then, of course, yet another spacewalk to get back inside, this time with the moon rocks and the camera, all to get back where he started. It's quite a schedule: planned down to the minute, for some tasks; rehearsed *ad nauseum*; written down on a wrist checklist because that's the only thing he'll have access to in the suit over those many long hours.

I think back to Mother in her lab coat, back at the clinic, taking notes about patients. "Mama always said, 'A dull pencil is better than a sharp memory.'"

"My mother had twelve children. So even when my father was home, she was too busy for aphorisms."

For the next orbit we watch the moon not as tourists or jaded voyagers, but as professionals, on a mission working. Picking out landmarks on the far side to pay attention to when the Block-D fires again to start Blondie's descent. Discussing those landmarks with Control. Dream, plan, reality: we are two thirds of the way there.

As we pass back in to radio blackout and start to wind down for the evening I notice Blondie has written on the first DESCENT page not words, but an unusual pattern of craters. "Is that the initial point?"

"I was making notes on the schedule, on that pass. I figured it would be best to get visual confirmation. And right below, there was this arrangement."

The cuff checklist is bent convex around a bracket—a flex of the pages to keep them together in weightless space. I study the sketch carefully; the ink looks dry but I'm taking no chances. "It does look...very unique."

"All the craters, all the patterns...everything is slightly different all across the moon, but there is a similarity to the differences. Especially on the far side. It is easy to get lost." Gingerly he takes the checklist back; he is taking no chances, either. "But this pattern is very striking visually. Perfect for our purposes."

"Like it was meant to be there." Outside again: the impossibly numerous stars, in infinite variations: size, distance, color. "Everything in nature is unique."

He scoffs. "Yes. Every water molecule, every atom of hydrogen..."

"Even then. I do believe it's all numbered, all known."

"By whom?" A long pause. "You are a believer, aren't you?" He goes on: "I see evidence of meteors. Not God."

"Everyone has faith in something. You have faith in the system."

"After our talk at dinner, you still think that?" He smirks. "I will say this. I can see the system. And my father was right, it does work. Very imperfectly, but it works. It always corrects itself eventually."

"It works for you. It corrects itself for you." A head shake. "It would be different, if you were me."

"You're here too. You're with me now."

We drift. The sun bursts through the window, far more intense than on Earth. Blinding in its brilliance, impossible to behold.

We study craters in silence. Looking again at patterns, trying to make sense of them. Then again he speaks. "So you are a Jew then? It's more than just...an answer on Line 5 of the passport form?"

I say nothing.

"Or...what? Don't tell me you've converted."

A glance at the radio button. Not only is it off, but we are cut off by the mass of the moon for a few more minutes. Nevertheless...would they record us? Read the transcripts? Would anyone care what I say here? Best not to chance it. Although I suppose we've both said things that could get us in trouble... "Would that be a more acceptable answer?"

He shrugs.

"I heard a rumor. That the day Gagarin flew, the KGB showed up at his parents' house. Not to arrest them or interrogate them. To sanitize it, before TASS showed up. Take all the icons and crosses off the wall. They were in a panic when they realized how excited the country was. It was the biggest thing that had happened since the war. Bigger than our satellite, even! He had to be a perfect Soviet man. He had to be a product of the system."

He sighs. "I heard that rumor too."

"You were closer to him than anyone."

"He was my friend! More than a friend. Especially after Sunrise-2. We both knew what it was like to be chosen." He shakes his head. "Still there were things I didn't know. And then, his crash was..." (A shudder.) "We had gone to the barber together, a week before. There was a...mole on the back of his neck. I told the barber, 'Careful, you'll nick that,' and he said, 'I'm always careful.' And Yuri said, 'Me too!' I didn't think anything of it. Then...the horror. The crash. I was in the air, doing parachute training. I heard two booms. I had a bad feeling, I didn't know why. Then, back on the ground...when they said his plane hadn't returned yet..."

I say nothing. What can I say? We both know about crashes. Down on the moon: craters upon craters upon craters. I spot the pattern from his checklist, the ones we're relying upon.

His mind is elsewhere. "There was nothing left at the crash site. Just...a twisted engine, aluminum debris. A smoking hole, surrounded by blackened trees. I've sketched it many times. There was hope he had ejected, that he was unconscious somewhere. When they determined which way the plane had been flying on impact, they were going to go backwards along its path, to see if they found him, if by some miracle he was...but then someone found scraps of his flying jacket, scraps of..." (Another shudder. He looks up at me.) "Someone put them in a surgical bowl. I looked in, and there was that mole. I told them they could stop looking."

"I'm sorry."

"But somehow it was worse afterwards. Because it was him. It was...inconceivable to everyone that a man who had been so lucky was..." (A head shake.) "So there were stories, there were rumors. I'm sure you heard them. They drove me crazy! Rumors he was drunk when he got in the plane before the accident. Rumors it was no accident, that he had... thrown a cognac in Brezhnev's face, and they'd staged an accident, so they could...throw him in prison anonymously, and no one would go looking. When you're on the outside, or even when you're on the edges, it always looks like there's some...great mystery, some grand conspiracy. But I knew. I was there. The system is always simpler than people realize."

"Are any of us products of the system, though? Scratch the surface of any...new Soviet man. Underneath you'll find...conspiracy theories. Suspicion. Superstition."

"Astrology. Religion."

I shake my head. "A fair point."

"We're circling the moon. But we're not far removed from...Rasputin." He smiles. "We're headed in the right direction, though. 'Our fate is not in our stars, but in ourselves.'"

"Shakespeare?" I smirk. "I would have expected a Great Russian. Pushkin, maybe."

"You think I'm Titov?"

I shrug.

"Very well. I think I have a verse in there somewhere." A long slow gaze out the window as the computer accesses its memory tapes. "Oh! Here it is." Then, as smoothly as if reading from a printout: "Then came a moment of renaissance. I look up: you again are there." And outside at this exact moment, as if summoned by his words, the bulge of blue comes rising into view. "A fleeting vision, the quintessence...of all that's beautiful and rare." Now: Earth above the barren horizon, intricate and glorious.

"Oh, come on!" Did he know his timing was going to be that absurdly precise? Is it an immense cosmic coincidence, or a masterpiece improvised in the moment?

No answers on his face: he just smiles and raises his eyebrows, leaving me alone with the silent mystery.

Still, I must admit I am impressed. "You know, I used to think..."

On crackles the radio. "Golden Eagle, Control. Come in, over."

"Control, Golden Eagle." Leonov answers on his headset. "Go ahead, over."

"Golden Eagle, we were waiting for you to say something. Do you have a status report? Over."

"Control, we've been taking stock of the past. And planning for the future. Yesterday was imperfect. Today was all right. No mistakes tomorrow. Over."

Perhaps I'm rubbing off on him. "No mistakes tomorrow," I echo. "As smooth as a peeled egg."

We stretch our sleeping bags across weightless space, cover up the windows to shut out the sunlight, pretending our clocks mean something out here: the day ending now, for night. Normal routines, taking turns at the urine tube. I expect him to stay up again, to take one of the covers down and spend a few minutes sketching the barren surface, now that we're so close. But he turns in at the same time as me.

A long heavy silence. Then: "Boris, I've been..." Hesitation: he looks at me across the gap.

"What is it, Alexei?"

"I've been..." The words stop; there is a changing of gears. "You know, you can call me Blondie, if you want to."

That wasn't good luck for Yuri, it occurs to me. But I do not say anything. There's no point in sabotage. Not when we're so close.

•••

"Wake up, sleepyhead! It's time to land on the moon!"

Leonov's voice, hateably optimistic. Before I can avert my eyes he removes the window covers. Again the morning sunlight, penetrating and all-consuming. Everything awash in golden light. The glory of God, impossible to behold.

But he's right. It *is* a beautiful day; no need to check the weather. Or the news, for that matter: we are making it.

He is making it.

"All right, all right." I blink, fully awake now. Clocks and cosmonauts may do their part, but the things that get you out of bed in space are the same things that do so on Earth: a busy to-do list, and a bursting bladder. Knuckles: I rub my face and eyes. Unzip my bag, pull myself out into empty airspace. "It was a very deep sleep."

"As long as you're awake when I get back! I won't be here to get you up. I will have to execute the rendezvous myself, and come knocking on the hatch. 'Boris! Boris! Let me in, Boris!'"

"Very funny." I grab the urine collection device for some desperate relief.

"It's a universal truth that people draw the sun yellow, when in fact it is white," he says as he finishes the breakfast packets. "Did you know that? Every culture. Yellow sun in a blue sky."

"Or orange. Like those Japanese prints."

"Yes, for the sunset maybe. But nobody draws it white, which is what it is, most of the time."

"I never thought of that." A glance out: still the far side. I am grateful now that he woke me when he did; a few more minutes and it might have been Control, asking me to push buttons and check settings with scarcely a *good morning*, and no respectful pause for the needs of biology. "So what color will it be in your moonscapes?"

He laughs. "We'll see how I remember it."

Below amongst the bright craters I see his pattern, the place where, in a few short hours, it will start for real, this thing that has already started. "You'll have pictures."

74

"A crutch." He hands me my sausages, a strange look in his eyes, like he's trying to get a reaction. Or am I imagining it?

We eat.

"It is a disappointing thing sometimes," he goes on. "To develop film after a trip. To see how flat the pictures look. How much the camera failed to capture."

"It certainly can be." I am thinking of a trip from a few years back. A shot of Andrei and I, taken by a stranger in front of the spaceship display at VDNKh: so many feelings missing. "I'm sure you'll do your best today."

A strange smile. "It does make you wonder. The sun. If everyone remembers it differently than it really is, why is that? Is there a collective consciousness? A collective unconscious?"

"What are you talking about?"

"Well it always seems strange to me that our eyes are not well-suited to look at our own sun. That we get blinded. Sunburned. You'd think we'd be better adapted to life on our own planet. Unless..."

I snort. "Are you saying we came from somewhere else?"

"It is something I wonder about. Perhaps we were forgotten here. Castaways. Or: a lost outpost of a spacefaring species. So ancient that on Earth all traces fell to ruin, or sank into Atlantis. But on the moon...sometimes I imagine I'll go down there and find something.

"Such as?"

"An old outpost of some sort. Covered in hieroglyphics. From aliens that were really our forefathers."

Is he jerking me around? "You can't be serious."

A chuckle, a smile. "It's no more absurd than believing in God."

"We had to come from somewhere. Even if this...ridiculous theory were true, who then made them? We have been created. By God, by the universe...call it what you will."

"Or we are the creators."

Earthrise out the window. On crackles the radio. "Golden Eagle, Control. It is a glorious day for the Soviet Union. Rumors are circulating. The whole world is waiting to see what we're going to do. Are you ready to get started? Over."

"Control, Golden Eagle." I take it upon myself to respond as Leonov starts disposing trash. "We are finishing breakfast. Our commander has been talking foolishness when you weren't listening. I am quite concerned about his mental health. There is still time to swap mission assignments..."

"Very funny," Leonov says, unsmiling.

•••

And now we are starting the day's work in earnest; I am stowing our sleeping bags and preparing the orbital module for decompression while he retrieves everything from the storage locker—golden-tan suit, liquid-cooled garment, fecal containment system—and starts stripping. Soon his golden-haired ass is hovering in front of me, far closer than

I'd like. Emblazoned on my retinas: not the memory I wanted from this trip.

"All right," he says. "Condom is attached. Time to get it on!"

I am put off by the absurd crudities, the stupid obviousness of the joke. "Time to put on your diaper, you mean."

An eclipse of the moon as he pulls up the fecal containment garment: thank God. Gingerly I tug at the edges, making sure nothing is folded improperly. "Looks good."

"Putting on the liquid-cooled garment."

The underclothing is delicate: cloth interwoven with plastic tubing. A kink, a rupture, and he will perhaps not be able to complete his moonwalk. But I watch carefully as I orbit his backside, tugging at the garment when it folds, making sure everything is positioned properly. "All good."

And now, the massive suit: hard aluminum shell and hinged backpack and integrated helmet. It is really going to happen. Did I ever really have the chance to be the first? If I did, the window is closing. I should be happier to be here for it: the second-most important man in the great adventure. Maybe if it wasn't him...

"All right. Keep an eye so it doesn't get pinched." Legs first, he starts working himself through the back. "In we go." He will be in there for quite a while, and there is a trace of hesitation in his voice.

Or is that my imagination? "So far, so good. Time for your tubing."

"Time for my tubing." He pauses, legs most of the way in, arms still out, and attaches the tube from the end of the condom to the lead tube from the urine collection bag. "I think it's good. Can you look?"

The indignity. Is he doing this on purpose? I push myself around so I'm floating upside-down now relative to him, hands and face far too near his crotch, an unfortunate approximation of the position the French call *soixante-neuf*. "Tubing looks good."

We hook up the water tubing as well, triple-checking the connections to the feed lines that snake around the interior of the aluminum suit torso. In truth it is almost like a miniature spacecraft in there. This thing that I'm seeing, it will see the lunar surface.

Then at last he is plunging his hands into the fabric-lined armholes and ducking his head into his suit like a swimmer eagerly plunging beneath the surface of a pool. His back remains, bare and exposed, filling the open hatch of the suit. And it occurs to me how much he has to trust me, how necessary I am to the success of this. There are any number of things I could do to sabotage the endeavor, but of course I do not do them: awareness is not desire. I would like this to succeed; I would like it as much as anyone who isn't Leonov.

I swing the hinged backpack closed carefully, making sure the levered locking mechanism engages, chatting now with Blondie—Alexei—over the headset. Everything was sized and fitted on the ground but now there are adjustments to be made, knobs to be turned, straps to be cinched so it is all just right, arms at the proper length for maximum dexterity of his gloved fingers. I pivot here and there, swinging my body through the empty air, correcting this and that until he and I are both content that everything is as it should be. Then the last piece, the over-the-shoulders chest display.

Finally I float back around to look at him one more time through the round helmet glass. My eyes meet his. "It looks like this is really happening, Blondie." I am surprised to hear the nickname on my lips. Is it bad luck? If so, for whom? My luck is his luck, for the next few days at least.

But his eyes betray no surprise. "It does appear that way."

I clap him on the shoulder—or rather, the hard edge of the suit torso—awkwardly; it seems appropriate, although I know he can't really feel it. "You've got this."

At last in those eyes, a sunlight twinkle. "I know."

I clasp his gloved hand, grip his suited arm with the other; here at last he can feel the reality of human contact despite the layers in between us; here at last I can feel it, too.

Then he pushes his visor down: no face now, but an impassive golden orb.

And I push myself back and away, pivoting around, scanning the orbital module again for anything we don't want exposed to the vacuum of space, anything loose we don't want drifting out once we open the hatch. It gives me some satisfaction to see that his sketchpad is in here; it has somehow floated free from its hiding place in the descent module. He surely cannot see it now, from inside his suit. If I do nothing there is a very real chance it will drift out the hatch once it's opened. All that artwork, made priceless and perfect by its absence...

But of course the invisible puppet strings of conscience are pulling my arms through the motions of retrieval. I float with the sketchpad back into the descent module, my only home for now.

Through the opening I can see his floating body hanging there, space-suited and larger than life: a dangling toy much bigger than the one hanging in my son's room, a grand prize. Or a mockup for the ones that will be on sale this summer, although surely for those he will not be floating free but upright, standing on a cratered plastic surface, planting a flag.

Assuming I see him again.

"Control, Golden Eagle. Suit-up complete. I am back in the descent module. Ready to close the hatch and depressurize. Over."

Two seconds of silence. "Copy, Golden Eagle."

The spacesuited body hangs there in the bright interior lights, faceless, oblivious to me now. At last it is eclipsed by the sickly green of the interior hatch.

•••

It is hard not to think about the problems he had on his last spacewalk, man's first. It was a harrowing experience—at least, that's what he told us.

The suit design was poor; it swelled up when he was out there, swimming alone in the empty universe. The most glorious visions he'd ever seen—the blue planet beneath, and sunshine on Sunrise-2—but when it came time to come inside he realized he had to exert tremendous effort just to move his arms and legs.

The spacecraft had been clumsily rigged with a flimsy external canvas airlock; because his suit had ballooned, he needed to let air out of the valves to deflate it just so he could squeeze back in head-first. But lowering the suit pressure risked decompression sickness, all the nitrogen in his blood frothing out painfully like bubbles from soda water. He had to take that risk, and he didn't say anything about it over the radio, so as not to alarm Control. At least, that's what he told us afterwards.

Then, because he'd had to squeeze back in the wrong way, he needed to reverse himself in the airlock to reach the controls. That took some work, and soon he was overheating. Sweat down to his knees, he said, although that part of the story always sounded the least plausible: Why would it pool down there in weightless space? Did he really stay in the suit all the way through reentry and only notice it on the ground?

He very nearly passed out, in which case he would have died. Belyayev could not have come out to rescue him.

He very nearly died. At least, that's what he told us afterwards.

Depressurization is complete. We are cut off from communications with Earth, passing through the moon's shadow, waiting for sunrise on the far side so the spacewalk can commence. We can only talk with each other, but we are not saying much.

What is happening now on the other side of the hatch? He is squeezing his hands, testing his grip. Checking range of motion, moving arms and legs, alone in the bright airless orbital module; our once and future home would now kill him in seconds. But he has all he needs so he is pleased, perhaps. Smiling to himself.

Sunlight in the windows.

"Coming out now."

There had been talk of having me out there with him in an Eagle spacesuit, guiding him out and then going out myself. Seeing infinity, open and free; looking down at the moon, close enough to touch; helping him through the hatch in the shroud that covers the Lunar Craft. But in the end it had seemed like too much risk, versus having me stay in the descent module. In the end even I did not think it was a good idea.

So I am stuck imagining the scene. And when I do I see that he has forgotten to clip in along the railing that leads to the instrument module.

He has forgotten, and there is a brief moment where his legs swing out and up, too much momentum leaving the hatch, and he cannot grasp the rail tightly enough with his fingers; his body is drifting now; he reaches, even though he knows it's too far; he kicks his legs like a swimmer, even though he knows it will make no difference. Nothing is going to kill him immediately; his suit still has hours' and hours' worth of oxygen. But he is floating free, and in a few hours he will die. He is embarrassed—such a stupid mistake!—so he asks me to turn off the radio relay to Earth so he can explain the situation to me, his relatively imminent demise. "No, you don't have to die," I tell him. "I'll come get you." With courage and confidence I maneuver the spacecraft closer. Edging nearer, straining to see out the portholes, mindful of the location of the thrusters. And if he is careful, he avoids the thrusters and grabs the railing, gratefully singing my praises; I have saved the mission. But perhaps he gets too close to a thruster (even though I have warned him!) and burns a hole in his glove and decompresses, and I go home alone. And in a few weeks I speak mournfully and warmly and falsely at his massive state funeral.

Unless I read the checklist: "Secure hook on exterior railing."

"Hook is already secure." One unnecessary word: *already*. And a tone in his voice: *as if I'd forget*.

Outside, sunlit moon under black sky, the pockmarked far side sharp and real. Am I seeing it as well as he is? Better? He has the whole spacecraft between him and the moon; I am looking sideways to the black horizon. My clothes are more comfortable, but his field of view is much greater. Surely he is taking a few moments to marvel at the sights, to feel—again—alone in the universe.

Next checklist item: "Equipment bag clear from hatch."

"Equipment bag is clear." Camera, film, two meals: everything that isn't already in the lander. "Moving along the railing."

The blind wall of the descent module blocks my view as he pulls himself past me, towards the instrument module and the rest of the spacecraft stack; I can only see him when I close my eyes.

He calls out: "End of the descent module."

Next item: "Second hook to instrument module railing."

"Clipped in." Clipped tones. But this is how it should be: checklist, confirmation.

"Release first hook."

"Hook released." Is he insulted by the reminders? It is my job to give them. Surely he can respect that.

A glance at the spacecraft clock, at our scribbled-in daysheet. We are coming up on earthrise. Not on the spacewalk checklist. Should I tell him? My reluctant conscience has been pulling my arms and legs as if I were a marionette on strings; now it ventriloquizes me. "Coming up on earthrise."

"Well that's worth a look from out here." Surely now he is lifting his golden visor, showing his face to the eager planet; surely many of them happen to be looking up right now, too, wondering if the rumors are true and we're about to attempt a landing.

"You're not going to quote Pushkin again?"

"A true artist never repeats himself."

And there it is now, the beautiful blue. A scene repeated countless times, unseen but by God. (*No God in Space*, the posters say, although from my perch it is easy to imagine someone watching over all this.) Does God need to look? Does God need anything, for that matter? Whom does it serve, to imagine God like us? An artist working for six long days to create a masterpiece like none other, then leaning back from the canvas to take it all in. How long would it take to truly see it all, to truly appreciate it, even as it changes from minute to minute? Perhaps a lot longer than that seventh day; perhaps God is still resting. Or: taking longer breaks now in his old age. Taking naps, even. For who could watch the hell of this cursed century and do nothing? Jews machine-gunned in forested ravines. Or: shipped across Europe on trains, like cattle. Next: separated on arrival, mothers and sons herded into showers, bare and shivering in the chill, huddled together for warmth, waiting for water from the showerheads, worried it will be colder still, unmindful of the vents until it is too late. Then: eyes wide with terror. Innumerable agonies, parents watching children gasping for breath, and vice versa. (Which would be a worse sight?) And at last the infinite finality. Bodies becoming corpses. Corpses desecrated, incinerated in ovens: whole families gone to ash. And soon on the other side of the globe: Japanese cities gone in a flash. American innovation putting German efficiency to shame. A glimpse of the future? We must not allow it.

And yet: they read from Genesis, the dead crew of Apollo 8. Surely they saw what we saw, what God saw: that it was good. (From a distance at least, with an artist's backwards lean.) Alexei may fantasize about our ancestors coming from elsewhere, but this dead desert below is no Eden. And if there is a Promised Land...

Earth crackles in our headset. Komarov, our guide until the end. "Golden Eagle, Control. Status on the spacewalk, over?"

"Control, Golden Eagle. Coming up on the shroud hatch," Leonov says. "Over."

He has a tool, a special torqueless socket wrench cinched tight on a tether. Did we check for it, during our inspection? Perhaps the tether has loosened; the tool has drifted off into space and is glinting in the distance, but soon we will be in darkness and it will be invisible, unrecoverable. And we'll be returning home in shame. No announcement from the State that it was anything other than an elaborate dress rehearsal, a necessary preparation for the "actual" landing mission, but everyone around Star City will know, will whisper amongst themselves, and stop whispering when we enter the room...

"First bolt removed."

Or not.

•••

Indicator lights: he is inside now, turning on the Lunar Craft.

When he removed the hatch, that interior space was dark, dead, metallic: a fearful mechanical cave. But now the lights are on and everything is familiar. Aluminum interior unpainted—every gram of mass counts!—and marred by rivets and welds. Controls and panels and indicators stuck here and there, all the tight mass budgets and careful design choices giving it an unfinished, haphazard look, function over form, quite unlike the sleek white lines of, say, an American sci fi movie. But surely it is beautiful to him.

He has pulled himself through the side hatch head-first and is now facing the round front window, through which he will create the most exciting scene in human history; currently it faces the inside of the launch shroud, scant centimeters away: bare bland metal, lit at a slant by the glow of the interior lights.

"Control, Golden Eagle." Speaking to Earth by way of our high-gain. "I am secure in the lander and the hatch is closed. Batteries are on and the electrical current is nominal. Guidance figures entered. Running environmental checks. Over."

For our benefit he narrates. From his cadence I envision: gloved fingers moving purposefully over the controls. Not slow, but deliberate. Stopping after each button press to consult the wrist checklist.

"Copy, Golden Eagle."

Will he tell us if something is off-nominal? If there is some minor problem in one of the systems Control can't monitor, big enough that it would give them pause if they knew about it, but small enough to make him think he can resolve it on his own? No. No, he will not tell us.

"O2 pressures nominal. Control system pressurized. Lander thrusters OFF. Ready to test lander control of the Block-D."

My cue. One of my few, in this phase. "Terminating control from the Orbital Craft."

"Controls activated. Testing Block-D control."

Outside I can see the bright lunar horizon start creeping downwards. Then it stops. He is in charge now.

From Earth, a muffled burst of static, garbled voices. "We've lost radio," I tell the one human who can hear me. The terminator pushes across the surface of the moon. We, too, will be in darkness soon.

"Is the high-gain on AUTO?" Managing my checklist as well as his.

"Ahh. Antenna to AUTO." A quick switch flip. I should thank him, but I do not.

"Golden Eagle, Control." Voices clearer now. "We lost you for a moment. Over."

"Control, Golden Eagle. Human error in the Orbital Craft." I owe them an acknowledgment, at least. "Lunar Craft is in control."

Outside, the sun is eclipsed by the moon.

At last their words make it back. "Golden Eagle, Control. Telemetry looks good. We have a functional moon lander. You are clear to separate on the far side and begin your descent. Over." Cheers in the control room.

"Congratulations to the Lunar Craft," I say flatly.

● ● ●

For each lunar orbit, four quadrants: sun, no radio; sun, radio; no sun, radio; no sun, no radio.

During the third of these, we listen as Control programs in the descent burn. For me, a brief respite. Some tidying up: grabbing binders that are now used and useless, stowing them up out of the way in the now-repressurized orbital module. Perhaps some museum on Earth would display them; perhaps some insane souvenir collector would cherish them; perhaps some rich American would pay many dollars for them. But they are destined to end up as trash on the moon.

Then: time for a bathroom break as we sweep into radio silence. Does he need one? Probably not. Who could think of bodily functions at a time like this, if they were in his shoes?

"Pretty quiet in there." Leonov in the headset.

"I have to answer the call of nature." I turn on the collection device vacuum so he gets the point. Soon it will be impossible to talk to him for long portions of my orbit. In truth I am thinking I won't mind.

Outside again, the star-stippled cosmos in all its nighttime glory. I remember at the last minute not to dump the urine; it won't sublimate in the darkness, and we don't want it interfering with the alignment sensors.

"Make sure you don't dump the urine," he says.

"As if I'd forget." The ass.

•••

"One minute to sunlight." Now the waiting is almost over.

"Arming x-axis translational thrusters. Standing by to separate."

"And…" Blinding sunburst through the windows. "Clear to separate."

"Copy, clear to separate."

A silent series of shudders passes through the spaceship, all timed in sequence by the brilliant engineers of OKB-1: pyrotechnic devices sending miniature guillotines through umbilical connections, explosive bolts firing, gas generator pushing the Lunar Craft backwards out of the shroud in a smooth steady motion.

What does he see? The bland view of the inside of a metal cylinder now sliding smoothly past, then giving way to sun or blackness or moon. The system working perfectly: small tremors in succession, and now it is spent. Almost orgasmic, although I am not pleased with the metaphor. I am hoping there will be a few moments of silence before…

Leonov: "That was almost orgasmic."

"That's another mental image I don't need." My angle is wrong to see anything, but soon that will change; I re-arm my thrusters.

"What's the matter with my description, Boris?" I can almost see the disgusting smile.

"The world will be listening soon."

"Yes, we don't want to tell them about our love."

"Let's keep it professional. You're clear from the shroud?"

"I'm clear from the shroud."

"Very well. Coming around." I start to pivot. Everything is nimbler now, a smaller and less massive spacecraft stack— a Union plus the launch shroud, and once I press a button, that will be discarded, too. And now I can see him, the top of the Lunar Craft pointed straight at me but receding slowly, the large wide docking plate gleaming in the sunlight; I count four shroud guides fluttering away. "Guides are all gone. Distance roughly twenty meters. You picked up some rotation. Clear to enable all thrusters and null out your rates."

"Enabling thrusters. I'll rotate so you can get a visual." With smooth movements he pivots his small spacecraft stack.

And...everything is as it's supposed to be, the lander's legs still folded, the lander perched firmly atop the Block-D. I will not see it flying by itself, let alone standing on its own; no one will see it, except him. "All right so far. Go ahead and deploy the legs."

"Deploying the legs."

More small pyrotechnics: one-time, reliable. The legs kick out in unison, away from the central truss that connects the lander to the Block-D. If there is a reason to delay or abort, I do not see it. "You're looking good!"

"You're looking good yourself, Eagle-2!"

The new call sign. Another reminder: if the window was ever open for me, it's certainly closed now. "Thank you." Too flat.

"Let's try to have some fun! You're lucky to be up here."

"That's what they keep telling me." Thoughts of the accident. A scan of the daysheet. "Block-D burn in five minutes."

"As if I'd forget."

"Keep an eye out for your craters, too."

"I will. Bye for now." In the lander's round window I can see a wave of his gloved hand: a childish gesture.

Still my hand comes up to the porthole: a quick wave of my own. "Good luck." Then I mutter something else, something like a blessing.

We orbit together. I translate high, watching the metal bug gleaming in the sunlight as it flies ass-first, perched precariously on its silly little platform. Far below, the rugged surface whips by, seeming faster now that it's set against a foreground. A scene of drama and urgency. I *am* glad to be a part of this; I am seeing things no one else will ever see, not even Alexei. I retrieve the movie camera and shoot a few precious moments of that delicate little insect flying backwards into the future.

"Coming up on the Block-D firing," he says. "Craters are below and it looks like we're on schedule."

"Copy, Eagle-1." This too has been programmed; we're out of sight, but Control is in charge. Still, it is nice to know we're on track.

"And...Block-D is firing. Right on schedule."

I wait for: what? Flame? Shudder? Explosion? There is perhaps a small mottling of the scene beyond the lander: it might be rocket exhaust, and might just be my imagination. But it has happened, the strange magic or orbital mechanics; he is dropping below me and drawing ahead.

•••

I am alone for earthrise.

Without him, the spacecraft is roomy; I can go to this porthole or that without the need to offer excuses or justify my existence in a particular piece of space. But it does remind me of Union-2—after the separation and before the troubles. A chilling thought...

"Eagle-2, Control." Komarov. "Give us a status. Over."

"Control, Eagle-2. Separation is complete and he is in descent orbit. You should pick him up shortly. Over."

We are doing something that has not been done. At least, not successfully.

Long silent moments. Then: "Eagle-2, Control. Still no communications. Can you reach him on the omni? Over."

"Eagle-1, Eagle-2. Come in, over." I imagine Leonov fumbling with the radio, overworked already.

"-2, this is -1." Calm and unhurried. "I'm getting static from Control. Over."

A message to relay. "Control, Eagle-2. I have him on the omni." All I'm needed for, for now. "He's picking up static from you. Over."

A longer gap than normal. Another link in the relay? Komarov consulting the engineers?

Finally: "Eagle-2, Control. What are his antenna angles? Over."

Another relay. "Eagle-1, Eagle-2. Where is your high-gain pointed? Over."

"-2, this is -1. Angles are...going back and forth a little. Over."

"It sounds like your tracking is off." Then, to Earth: "Control, Eagle-2. Tracking issues on the lander. Over." A moment of satisfaction: I am the linchpin. In the radio delay I can practically hear the murmurs on the ground: *Boris is on top of it! We're lucky to have him up there.*

A long pause. "Eagle-2, describe the issues. Over."

"Control, his antenna's going back and forth. Over."

Wait. Then: "Eagle-2, Control. Have him take the antenna off AUTO. Set pitch angle to minus ten degrees. Yaw plus fifteen. Over."

"Eagle-1, Eagle-2. Take your antenna off AUTO. Pitch minus ten. Yaw plus fifteen. Over."

Again the wait. Some worry. Then it occurs to me: they are talking on the other channel. I will have to listen in on the relay circuit now.

I switch over: "...gle-1, Control, we are picking up data now..."

And now they know the pressures in the thruster system, the voltage and amperage in every circuit. Are there issues Leonov lied about? Ones he brushed past? If so, he can no longer conceal them. But what will they do? Half an hour until landing: I can see them trying to push through it—or him ignoring them, putting the Lunar Craft on manual and pushing through anyway—pushing our luck right into a disaster. Or: what? Aborting the landing? Sending him home empty-handed, rewarding me for my honesty and experience with…

"…and the data is looking excellent. Clear to continue descent. Over."

"Control, Eagle-1. Continuing descent. Over."

They no longer need me. It is now my job to shut up and stay off the radio. I can practically see the smug smile on Leonov's face.

Silver dreams. The craters must be much larger for him now, everything whipping by faster and faster; already he has seen the moon better than anyone but Stafford and Cernan. Window pointed downwards, watching it draw near. Trusting Control isn't flying him into a mountain.

"Eagle-1, data is intermittent now. Let's go back to AUTO on the high-gain. Over."

"Copy, Control. AUTO on the high-gain. Over."

Darkening features below us now, Langrenus in the middle distance to the south: we are coming up on the Sea of Fertility, skirting its northern "shore" as we fly west. My Orbital Craft back in the thermal control roll; on one side I can see clear across Fertility, and to the north, much of the Sea of Crises. Langrenus is huge, with sunlit terraces rippling down to a wide flat floor and a bright central cone. To its northwest: three smaller craters in a rough triangle; they are becoming my favorites. How many more times will I see them? Less than ten, unless I come back again. They slide backwards out of sight.

"Eagle-1, Control. We show two-three-zero-four meters per second. Altitude thirty-five thousand. Fifteen minutes to perilune. Over."

"Copy, fifteen minutes."

Long slow silent minutes. Little for me to do except to follow along in the procedures binder, standing by in case he has to abort the landing. But they will not call an abort. And if they do, he will not listen.

Now, Taruntius, dominating the scrap of bright highlands separating Fertility from Tranquility. I imagine Blondie firing the Block-D early, swooping low, finding the crash site. Seeing: what? A lander, cracked but recognizable? Bodies inside, suits ruptured on impact—or intact, no way to tell Earth what had happened. Alone for minutes? Hours? Days? More likely: a small crater, twisted pieces of metallic debris. Scorch marks on the moon, perhaps; their hypergolics would have exploded once the tanks ruptured, never mind the lack of atmosphere. Bodies desecrated, perhaps just scraps. An American flag patch: red, white, blue, and blackened edges...

But no, we've seen enough crash sites. More than enough.

Tranquility gives way to the last bit of highlands. Craters and rilles, more interesting than where we're going. The Middle Bay drifts lazily by.

At last: "Eagle-1, Control. Altitude: twenty thousand. Rolling you upright. Over."

"Maneuver complete. Over." His distant voice, flat and professional, even less expressive than Control.

Then: the longest and most pregnant pause of all. And at last: "Eagle-1, stand by for final descent. Over."

"Copy, Control."

It is really going to happen. The last firing of the Block-D, the one that will finally slow him enough for the moon's gravity to pluck him out of what has been a low elliptical orbit. No time to strap in: I stop the thermal roll with the starboard porthole pointed moonward. Then: straining at the glass, looking for a glint of light; I'll be catching up with him soon.

"Control, Eagle-1. Initiating final descent. Over."

I strain to see: something. A sunlit speck still moving against the distant surface. The lander still perched on its short metal stool, preparing to leap off and flex its legs for landing. I see nothing.

"Passing through fourteen thousand. Block-D is firing. Over."

The engine has restarted: kerosene and liquid oxygen, safe as baby's milk. Pushing against the lander as it slides down the hill. Leonov inside, strapped upright, center of mass, ready for the Ocean of Storms. Window black with space, though he's probably not looking.

"Eagle-1, burn is looking good," Control says. "Ten thousand meters. Over."

"Copy, ten thousand meters."

How accurate are the altitude readings right now? How accurate can they be, from Earth?

"Five thousand meters. Coming up on Block-D separation. Over."

"Copy, five thousand."

He cannot see the moon rushing up beneath him. Too low, wrong readings. A metallic meteorite plowing an oblong crater in the surface of the moon...

No.

"Eagle-1, coming up on four thousand. One hundred meters per second. Initiating Block-D separation. Over." Behind it, a heavy silence: a roomful of people all holding their breath. The last command, although he could have done it on his own. Engineers and cosmonauts, all of us spectators now.

"Copy, Control. Arming lights lit." Brightness in his voice now. From the machine: another shudder. What does he see outside? Small bits of debris, fanning out in an arc? But he is not looking out; he is scanning the instruments, finding reassurance in familiar patterns. "And...clean separation. Block-E is firing. Lander is in control. AUTO mode."

I have memorized the diagrams: the Block-E separating the lander from its now-useless perch, the Block-D sailing onwards on its slanted trajectory, tossed onto the lunar surface like an empty can of Zhiguli on a Black Sea beach. I can see none of it but I am straining at the glass. The closest spectator.

"Block-E still firing. Pitching forward and I can see the surface. No landing radar."

A tense inhale, one I'm sure will be repeated a second later across the control room. I'm surprised he admitted it. This is an automatic abort if it persists.

"Still no radar. Surface getting larger. Seeing some craters. Cycling breakers."

My hand clenches a small fixture next to the window. Fingers tight, knuckles white. What if they call it?

"Eagle-1, abo…"

"Radar is on! Altitude two thousand. Craters are big. Still on AUTO."

I am insane. Did they call an abort, and he talked over it? They must have called it, two seconds ago. My hand clenches tighter. I did not know how much I cared.

"One thousand now."

The wait. Are they going to go with it? Then: "Eagle-1, call your fuel."

"One hundred seconds. I can see the landing point. Side of a large crater."

He can land on thirty degrees of slope. At least in theory. Filmstrip footage: a boilerplate lander plopping down awkwardly, nesting rockets firing to keep it steady on the surface. But who knows the properties of lunar soil? Easy to imagine dust giving way, the lander toppling, rolling to the bottom, exploding…

"Eagle-1, you're high. Over."

"Sixty seconds. SEMI-AUTO. Boulders on the crater floor. I think I can make the rim."

Drumbeats in my head. An invisible orchestra. Prokofiev.

"Thirty seconds. Still too far."

Sunlight behind him. A bright stone wall rising up in front. Rim too high now. The Block-E stage will be used for ascent as well. But if he uses too much fuel on the landing...

"Nulling out rates. I'll head for the center. Steer around the boulders."

The longest pause. Control can force the abort. Jettison the legs, throttle the Block-E to full...

"Eagle-1, give us a reading."

"Thirty meters. Heading straight down."

The rim rising higher. Above the window now? What is the fuel? He never said fuel.

"Eagle-1, you are negative fuel."

"Ten meters. Drifting back into shadow."

He did say boulders. A footpad on one and the lander flips over...

"Eagle-1, abo..."

"Picking up dust." An electric chill, hearing those words. Again he talked over them. I almost don't mind.

"Eagle-1! You are neg…"

"Contact!"

We did it!

"Block-E stop. Nesting rockets firing."

He did it.

"Lander is stable, systems are safe. It is May 15th, 1970, and we are on a crater floor in the Ocean of Storms."

"Eagle-1, Control. We copy you down." Cheers in the control room behind Komarov. "I will take my finger off the abort button." Even I can hear his smile. "Congratulations to the lunar lander."

Below I can see the blank scene scrolling by, this vast new ocean. Darkness approaching. He used too much fuel. Control will have to recalculate the rendezvous, send me into a lower orbit; we'll be much tighter on our margins. But that is a problem for later.

"Yes, congratulations," I echo, too late. No one is listening to me.

I unclench my hand, flex my fingers, wipe my eyes. Perplexing tears. Still they flow, unbidden. He is down. We are down.

●●●

A leisurely bathroom break in the lunar night, once I remember my bladder. Control is ignoring me. I can hear their instructions and discussions of system pressures and switch settings; I cannot hear his responses, for I am below his horizon now. Should I switch channels, ask them to put me on relay? No.

Earth disappears.

I am alone. Thinking again of Union-2, the calm before the calamity. Still I enjoy a long silent lunch: sausages and tea, staring out at the blackness and the bright infinity.

Nighttime walks in the forests around Star City: strands of birch, trunks painted soft blue by the moonlight. This same moon. God is there in the silence, the small whisper. And here: the hum of pumps and the whir of fans, pushing water and air through coolant loops.

For a few moments I am content. For a few moments there is peace.

Then my thoughts get stuck, flow backwards. What does he see? The round window, the looming crater face. Boulders on the floor near him—how big, how close? He will tell us in the debriefing, after the return, how close we were to disaster. Perhaps he is raising his camera to document the scene. The snap of the shutter and the mechanical ratcheting as he winds to the next frame. But no: the Lunar Craft is still unpressurized. No sounds but his breathing, and Control yammering in his ear. I can imagine him turning off the radio, just standing there in peace for a few moments, because what can they do now, to punish him? What can they possibly do?

But no, he is talking. And...are they announcing the landing? They must be, by now. The television camera waits on the leg of the lander. They are testing the signal, adjusting the antenna angles one degree at a time. Across the globe, the news anchors are reading the hasty printouts from their teletypes while their assistants comb their hair and apply pancake makeup. A nervous energy to it all: When will there be a story better than this?

And I sail through the darkness of the far side, apart from it all.

•••

He is getting ready to leave the lander.

I am coming up on sunlight, and no communications. I am supposed to be taking pictures of various lunar features so the scientists can gain support for this theory or that, volcanic action or lunar accretion. So many things I promised to pay attention to, so I could make it up here.

He is getting ready but he doesn't need much preparation; he suited up this morning, with me. And he's been getting ready on his own, for who knows how long. Words he has composed but not revealed. Words I will not hear.

I want him to succeed, of course. Even the strongest rivalries fade when you are working together on a shared goal, as long as there is some reluctant agreement about how it will be accomplished. Even Korolev and Glushko came together in the former's last months; even that happened, for the sake of this.

Still I can't help thinking: we had transmission problems the other day. What if they persist?

The rounded hatch opens in the side of the Lunar Craft. Viewed from the outside: a distorted dark crescent, although hopefully no one can see it except my mind, and God's. Inside, the inverse: the lander's recesses made darker by contrast with the sunlit scene outside.

All across the U.S.S.R., citizens are tuned in. For the lucky few with TV sets: Soviet Central Television, First Programme, beamed to the Far East by the Lightning satellite system. Others are turning radio dials, threading the needle through squelches and squeals to pick up Yuri Levitan, back on the air after all these years. "Attention, this is Moscow speaking…" for old times' sake.

Leonov kneels on the floor, a secular prayer. Normally a pose of humility, but not today. I saw enough of his training—and Bykovsky's—to know how the rest goes: the slow backwards shuffle on hands and knees. During simulations: anxious to get it right, pinched and claustrophobic but not letting on. And today: marveling at the realness, at the lightness of movement in one-sixth gravity. Thinking how little stands between the present and immortality.

Now he is coming out. Legs swinging lazily over to the ladder. Torso and then helmet and arms emerging. The bright expanse. Impossible to see where he is going, so he places each foot carefully. If he slips off a rung, he might crack his helmet faceplate on the top of the ladder. But nobody wants that; surely even the Americans don't want that.

They are tuned in now, along with the world. But what can they see? Grainy images, suit-clad legs against the black sky.

Or: a blurry ghost. The image not quite good enough, so they are fiddling pointlessly with the television antennas, unable to fix a problem that's hundreds of thousands of kilometers away. Perhaps the camera pointed during landing at the unrelenting sun; perhaps the circuitry's fried. Or: the bracket broken, despite all the testing; the camera dangling, lens pointed skyward, the field of view just a circle of black.

That would be too bad.

He makes his way down deliberately at first, then with exuberance in inverse proportion to the number of rungs left on the ladder, for there is very little left that could go wrong. He stands for a moment on the lander's footpad; he tests the soil with a single boot. There it is! He has touched the moon! All those alarmist theories: dust like quicksand, ready to swallow him whole the second he steps off. He already thought they were wrong; now he smiles, for he knows for sure.

Then: one step. Two steps.

Words. Famous words we will all soon know by heart. Man's glorious conquest, this bold new experience, narrated by a Magellan brave enough to make the ultimate voyage alone, and yet generous enough to share it in real time with the waiting world. And: some claptrap about Lenin, a sop to the party hacks. Wooing a woman you've already won; kind words to your jealous wife so she knows you won't leave her even now, now that you're famous and could have anyone. Beautiful lies, although perhaps they feel true today, even for him. For surely it's all forgiven now: his father's imprisonment, Stalin's excesses. Yes, Lenin—far better. The centennial of his birth just past: the propaganda writes itself. Lenin to Leonov, a hundred years of progress. A new birth for mankind.

And yet no one can see it, for the camera is broken.

Wouldn't that be too bad?

•••

"Control, Eagle-2, coming around the far side." Another earthrise, less lonely now. "I hope you haven't forgotten about me. Over."

The wait. And: "Eagle-2, are you still up there? Over."

I laugh; I don't even mind. It does feel good to be a part of this. "Control, I thought about flying elsewhere while everyone was distracted. But I decided to stick around and see how it's going. Over."

In the delay now there is a moment of suspense before the confirmation: "We've done it! He's outside!"

A flood of: some emotion. "Fantastic! I'll send my congratulations once I'm overhead."

"It's all going well except the television. The camera seems to be broken."

My absurd prophecy coming true. I am not quite sure how to feel, or what feelings to admit to. "Well I hope he takes plenty of pictures."

"I'm sure he will, Eagle-2."

Photography time for me as well: my flight plan calls for more shots of prospective landing sites. I do want to do this well; hopefully for more than selfish reasons, although certainly there is that thought, that the work I do now will be guiding me down in a year or two. Fertility: another unknown sea. Perhaps worth visiting: the scientists would certainly like lunar soil from a range of places, and the larger impact craters will give us a chance to sample lunar bedrock. So perhaps my three small satellite craters, or Langrenus itself...

"Eagle-1, that's quite an interesting description." Half the conversation, on this channel. "We're all looking forward to seeing it up close. Over." Komarov: eager to share in the triumph? A potential rival for me, later on? Both?

I could, if I wanted, have them patch me in to the communications relay, to hear both sides of the conversation. I am curious as to what the moon looks like for him, given how its color changes from up here: gray when the shadows are long, more tan in the areas of high sun. He'll be packing most of the rocks in a vacuum-sealed sample box, so I won't see them any time soon, although I will perhaps catch a glimpse of the initial sample bag of soil, the hasty scoop he's already collected in case he has to lift off early...

Back to the task at hand. A roll of film finished, rewound, changed. Documented on the flight plan so the photography team can sort through it all later. Not like a normal vacation—we won't be developing these rolls in a home darkroom!

More pictures of my trio of craters. Rough terrain between them: would it be possible to set down in the middle and visit all three on one mission? There was talk of landing a

Moonwalker rover separately from the Lunar Craft but close enough to reach on foot; if I talk them into resurrecting that plan I could use it to reach spots that would otherwise be too distant. Standing on the front of the rover, using hand controllers to steer it this way or that across the lunar surface…now that would be an accomplishment, being the first person to drive on the moon!

"Eagle-1, we have a distinguished guest who would like to speak to you. Hold one moment…" A switching of signals, a moment of suspense; a voice more distant, but clear. "Comrade Leonov." Brezhnev. "It is a great privilege to be speaking to you on the first telephone call to the surface of another planet. We have a few surprises in store for you. But first: the people of the Soviet Union, our fraternal socialist allies, and indeed all of humanity join us in congratulating you on this accomplishment, a triumph you have made alone on our behalf. Just as Comrade Lenin's birth one hundred years ago heralded an era of progress for the world's workers, so your landing on the moon is a sign that our potential is unlimited. A generation ago, the Soviet Union led the world in the fight against oppression and backwardness and rapacious capitalistic cruelty. Now you and your comrades in the cosmonaut ranks are engaged in a new struggle, a fight to lead the world forward into a new age of reason and rationality, science and shared humanity. You have already done much; it was my great privilege to bestow upon you the title Hero of the Soviet Union after your Sunrise flight. Now it is an even greater privilege to speak to you today and announce that you are a Hero of the Soviet Union twice over. Thank you for your service to the nation, General Leonov!"

General? Is he drunk? Or… (In the delay, my dread grows.)

"Yes, that was the other surprise! Congratulations on your promotion."

A pause. More words from the other end, no doubt. Am I glad I can't hear him? God, he'll be insufferable now.

Laughter from Brezhnev. "Very well, then! Yes, that's quite a good idea!"

Another long pause.

"Yes, we are looking forward to seeing you and your crewmember. I am sure it will be less eventful than the last time!"

Memories: crowds, shots, screams. Amazing he'd mention it, even obliquely. A bad omen? He must be drunk.

"Yes, of course, I am very eager to hear you share what you saw on this fantastic voyage. I am sure I speak for the world in wishing you and your crewmember a safe return."

Your crewmember. No name.

And now it seems the call is over.

Your crewmember. He's met me! And yet…

I breathe, relax, shake my head. I am a part of this, even though for the moment it doesn't feel that way; I am a part of it, and without me it will fall apart. There is no small comfort in that.

What is he doing down there? There are a handful of experiments to deploy. Not many: a laser reflector for measuring the distance to the moon, a seismometer for detecting lunar quakes. I saw a little of the training: first Bykovsky, then him. For all he cares they could be empty shoe boxes he's discarding on the moon...

There is also the flag. Our crimson banner, limp and lifeless. Is the lander in the sun, or sunk in the angled shadow of the lunar crater? Either way it would make for a good picture. Too bad there's no one to take it! Surely he's trying anyway, holding the camera at arm's length, trying to get the angles right, clumsily dropping it, fumbling as it falls slowly to the lunar soil, wishing there had been room in the mass budget for a tripod and a timer. There's only so much you can do yourself, comrade...

"Eagle-2, this is Eagle-1. Come in, over."

Our communications window! It snuck up on me. Almost thirteen minutes, and I've pissed away...how many? "Eagle-1, Eagle-2. Go ahead. Over."

"Just making sure you hadn't forgotten about me! Over."

"Who could forget about you, Comrade General?" Floating back to the periscope: I am supposed to at least attempt to locate his landing site.

"Ahh, yes, you were listening!"

"Everyone was listening, Comrade General." Does sarcasm transmit over radio waves?

"Eagle-2, I won't insist on that level of formality. You can simply call me General!"

Against my will, I laugh. "Very well, General." I'm at the eyepiece now, scanning lunar craters as they drift by. Powerful magnification, narrow field of vision: how many inevitable tradeoffs there are in life! "I'm trying to spot you through the periscope. No luck yet. Over."

"Eagle-2, in all seriousness, I know I could not have done this without you."

"Or someone like me!"

"Eagle-2, it is true. Others on Earth may have forgotten, but I will make sure to remind them. You are an essential part of this. Over."

"Eagle-1, you're just saying that because you need me to fly you home! Over." Still my heart warms, against my better judgment.

"Eagle-2, I do mean it. Looking forward to seeing you later. Over."

"I'm sure you are. I'm sure you are." At last I remember: "Congratulations on your accomplishment, Alexei. I'm looking forward to hearing all about it."

No response. Did he hear? I must be over the horizon now, which also means there is no need to keep searching. A mild annoyance: it would have been nice to brag about. Although if the lander was in shadow, it might have been an impossible task.

Somehow now I am picturing him not in his spacesuit on the moon, but in uniform, hanging up the phone after our talk. Laden with medals, a rippling golden cascade, more than

Yuri had, even. After the Great Patriotic War there were others like that: Zhukov reviewing the victory parade up on the mausoleum with Stalin, chest heavy not just with gold but the knowledge of all the blood that had been shed to earn it. (And perhaps fear: a keen awareness that the man with the moustache did not want anyone to outshine him.) Perhaps this is better. A peaceful triumph. Although not without cost...

The terminator sweeps beneath me across the surface of the moon. Fuzzy, but final. Again I listen to half-conversations: Control monitoring his progress, monitoring his heart rate, monitoring the level of oxygen in his tanks. Alexei performing like a trained bear at the circus, happy to get out of his cage and be the center of attention. Whereas I get to stay in there, unmolested. My spacecraft is flying perfectly; there is nothing for me to do.

At last, the words stop, mid-sentence. Solitude, not loneliness. Floating alone in the starlit darkness. I am in control, more control than Alexei; no human can monitor me. Still the invisible strings drag me along this fixed path, this set course.

●●●

It is time for him to collect pieces of the moon.

The sample box is stored on the side of the lander. A rounded aluminum container, a squat metallic suitcase. He disengages the latches; one is stuck. But no, it comes loose once he gets his gloved fingers all the way under it, and the box falls lazily to the lunar soil.

And now he is toting it around the crater, grabbing up rocks. Basalts? Breccias? He knows the difference, and I know that he knows, and that's all I know. (My training was different: a couple classroom sessions with Makarov, before the accident; a geologist showing us photos from the circum-lunar flight so we'd know the different types of craters and mountains and rilles.)

Basalts: that is most likely. I do remember that.

He is grabbing up rocks, trying to get a "representative sample," or whatever it was the geologist said. How many different types can he see on the crater floor? The boulders: Are they native to the crater, or were they thrown there as ejecta from some other collision? And how long ago: a million years, or last week? He is striking one with the sharp end of the rock hammer, breaking off a piece, depositing it into a numbered sample bag. But I know this is the part of the mission he is least enthusiastic about; he's going through the motions because they told him he needed to. Hopefully the geologists are listening in on the radio loop and taking good notes.

And now, looking around: he decides to climb out of the crater.

Maybe he tells them he wants to get rock samples from the rim; surely he's just eager to see what he can see. Control does not like the idea but he reassures them; he tells them he can see a way up that looks stable. Not a path, for of course nothing is a path down there, not yet. But he thinks he can get up there safely on the side with the shallowest slope, or maybe the side with the most sun. Walking slowly the whole time, perhaps poking the ground ahead with the sample scoop to make sure it is stable.

Anyway they cannot stop him.

He goes halfway up before stopping to grab a quick sample. Still it is not steep. That's what he tells them, anyway.

He presses on, a few more steps up the slope. Used to the strange gravity now, the way the bulky suit moves. How steep is it? Still shallow enough to walk? Maybe he has to put his hands down to steady himself. Can they tell from his heart rate how hard he is working to get up there? Do they say anything?

Surely things will start to go wrong, sooner or later.

And sure enough: he slips. Smashes his faceplate on a rock. Hears the whooshing rush of air, gasps pointlessly for breath, feels the ice crystals forming at the corners of his eyes as his vision fades...

No. No, I do not want that. Even for him I do not want that.

He catches himself, steadies himself with one gloved hand, then the other. Does something like a pushup but fails to get his feet beneath him. Tries again and succeeds. Moving more carefully now, he makes it the last few meters up to the crater rim. Tests his footing. Hops up. Takes a few steps from the edge to make sure he's on stable soil. Stands alone up there, and surveys the endless emptiness.

What does he see, down there on the Ocean of Storms? Craters—more of them, but how big? (We were able to estimate the size of the larger lunar features based on simple spherical geometry and their shadow length at sunset, but photographic resolution has its limits.) And how far does he walk from the big crater's rim? Far enough to let it eclipse the lander at the bottom. Far enough to only see his own footprints behind him. Far enough to look in the other direction and see nothing but moon.

Does he take pictures? No—he must have left the camera and the sample box halfway up the crater side so he could have an easier time with the climb. So he just lifts the golden outer visor, to see it as it actually is. Then he stands there and stares, so he can draw it later.

Perhaps he kneels at that farthest point. (Can he kneel? Yes, of course, he had to do so to get out of the lander.) Perhaps he writes his name in the dirt. GENERAL ALEXE—no, that would be absurd even for him, though I do smirk imagining it. Instead, ALEXEI LEONOV in large simple letters. Or just LEONOV. Or just ALEXEI.

Maybe one of the letters is not to his liking; he erases it with a swipe of the glove, even though no one else will ever see it. Then he tries again a few meters away. And once it is done he leans back and smiles, for he sees that it is good. The first human to sign the moon.

Now we just have to get him back.

The Thirteenth Cosmonaut

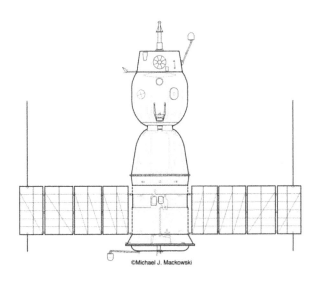

©Michael J. Mackowski

What does it mean to be lucky?

In my career, for instance—surely most people would say I should feel fortunate to be where I am. Or just to be alive after so many years; others—Bondarenko, Gagarin, Bykovsky, Makarov—cannot say the same. Some had substantial triumphs, accomplishments I envied; all are now in the ground.

But given all that happened on my way to the moon, I do not know what it means to be lucky. I just know my story matters. Everyone wants Leonov's story. But mine means something, too.

• • •

My birthday is December 18th. Right around Stalin—my fellow Sagittarius—which as a young boy seemed like a blessing, and later on felt like something else.

I spent my twenty-sixth birthday alone in the isolation chamber. I had been a normal pilot in a line unit, savoring my time alone in the cockpit, dreading the politics and prejudices I faced on the ground. Eventually I was recognized as the best in my regiment at rough-field takeoffs and landings, steering my silvery MiG down long dirt roads and into the sky, a skill which earned me plenty of pats on the back. (Which was a welcome change from the backstabbing.) But on my twenty-sixth birthday I was alone, striving for something more. I had not given my wife any inkling that I was seeking this new path; I had not sought her counsel. I had simply sent her away, back to the East. I have learned the hard way: I only seek my own advice.

The isolation chamber meant long periods of absolute silence. Electrodes clinging annoyingly to shaved patches of skin. Fixing food on a hot plate and working on number puzzles while being scrutinized or ignored—who could say?—by the men on the other side of the glass. Then: interrupted by alarms, random blasts of light and sound designed to set the heart rate racing, all so those in the other room could scan the results and note their disapproval.

Everyone had to endure the isolation chamber, for periods ranging from ten days to two weeks. (The fact that you didn't know how long it would be—that was part of the experiment.) I alone had to endure it on my birthday. They were eager to get in one more test before the holidays, before Grandpa Frost and New Year's. They had every piece of information imaginable on everyone; they could have picked Leonov (or anyone, really), but they picked me. And I was stuck in there, unable to so much as send a letter to my wife to let her know. That was the first humiliation.

●●●

I did not think I would be picked for East-1. I was at least spared that illusion. There were six in the running, and then it was just Gagarin and Titov and Nelyubov, and then it was just Gagarin and Titov. And we all know how that went.

I will admit, they made a good decision—Korolev and Kamanin, and the rest of the State Commission. They made the right decision. Even I will admit to that.

•••

East-5 found me riding the bus to the launch pad. I was backing up Valery Bykovsky, but I knew there was still a chance I'd fly. As it turned out, it would be a large chance indeed.

But I did not know that yet.

We were on the same blue-and-white bus Gagarin had ridden, and we were suited up in orange SK-1 flight suits, just like he had worn on his hundred-and-six-minute ride to immortality. June sun on the endless steppe, that lifeless arid place where even if, God forbid, we had an unlucky Seven—one that turned earthward and plowed into the ground at full speed, a kerosene-and-oxygen conflagration turning all that finely machined aluminum into blackened twisted strips—chances are nobody would be hurt, and the endless flat earth would not only absorb the blow, but forget about it within the month.

We were silent on the bus, that rumbling ride down the dusty steppe road, not all that different from the ones I'd landed on in my MiG. We were silent, and I remember glancing up at Bykovsky, watching him watch the emptiness roll by. It was not hard to read his thoughts; he was thinking about the future. Whereas I was mired in the past. The State Commission's final decision, three days before: such a bitter blow! Everyone knew the program was coming to an end. How long would it be now?

At last the bus lurched to a halt. He got up, beaming a self-satisfied smile; we were twins no more. All of the people and all of the activity: it was about to follow him off the bus. Except for me: I was to stay and wait. A bitter role: a supporting player in the movie of his life. Trained every bit as well as he was, but apparently destined for a less dramatic ride: an anticlimactic reversal of the bus trip, rather than a fiery and glorious ascent.

I wished him good luck, of course. He paused and reached back, almost as an afterthought, and our gloved hands gripped in supposed solidarity, like athletes on rival teams after a bitter game. I said, "Good luck, Valery," and his eyes darted away; he barely gave a reply. Did he know it was a lie?

There was a ritual, supposedly started by Yuri, to urinate on the tire of the transfer bus before ascending the rocket to the stars. Despite the angle of the windows I could see Bykovsky was carrying on the ritual, the clot of people around him giggling and looking elsewhere as he stood fixed in place, giving that contented look. I wondered absently how Tereshkova was going to pull it off in two days.

Then everyone—engineers, technicians, doctors, even the film cameraman—moved around him as he made his way to the launch pad stairs, as he ascended to the launch pad elevator and then turned and waved before getting on. It was his big day.

I had to wait. Alone with the endless emptiness.

It was cold, surprisingly cold. The bus had a fancy air conditioning system and they'd left it on, full blast. And my suit had a tank of compressed air to keep me ventilated, to keep me at the right temperature, but after a half hour, it ran out. And no one was paying attention to me. I thought about studying the checklists, perusing the flight plan for the mission I was now not taking. But what was the point? It was like sitting in the examination room at the doctor's. Just sitting there. Waiting. Real life happening outside— everyone taking action and making decisions. But inside the room? Nothing to do but wait.

I could at least see outside the bus; I could see the comings and goings at the base of the launch pad. But that made it worse. The sound on the movie had gone out. And my role was over, and everyone seemed quite content with that. I couldn't nap; I hadn't slept well but I was not quite tired. So I watched that boring movie for two full hours, and I was just about to draw the bus window curtains and bring the show to a close.

But then: an unexpected plot twist.

A figure, a doctor, climbed down the green metal stairs at the base of the launch pad and walked straight towards the bus. He climbed on, and I lifted my head to listen.

"Get yourself ready. We're going to have to swap him out. Bykovsky will not fly. You will fly."

Electrifying news! My pulse quickened; the day, bright and boring just a minute before, now swelled in significance. I *did* need to study the flight plan again; I *did* need to review the checklists. June 14th, 1963: a monumental day after all. Everything now suddenly seemed fascinating—the high summer sun casting small shadows on the short brownish grass and the cracked concrete and glinting off the railway tracks down which had rolled the mighty rocket. Today is the day, and this is the place.

Another man, an engineer, came down and explained the issue: a faulty gyroscope on the uppermost stage. There had been talk of taking the whole rocket down and draining the propellants; that seemed the safer bet after what had happened to Nedelin. But Sergei Pavlovich had apparently insisted: do the work in place. We're not dealing with hypergolics; we're not dealing with the devil's venom. This is kerosene and liquid oxygen. Safe as baby's milk.

So they were doing the work in place, fuel tanks full, and meanwhile another tank was filling, the urine bag in Bykovsky's suit, swelling and filling despite the ritual emptying of the bladder, and it would be unhygienic to launch him with a full urine bag; the tubing, the connection with the collection condom, was sure to come undone, especially once the g-forces started building during the rattling ascent. So they were going to launch me. They were going to have to launch me.

"How is your bag?" the engineer asked.

"Fine, not bad at all. I didn't have much tea this morning. I had a feeling all of this would take a while."

"Good. That is good. We're going to swap you out soon."

He returned to the pad. I watched his back as he ascended the long green staircase to the launch elevator, the same trip I'd be making soon, God willing. At last I undid the zipper in my SK-1; my own bag was, in truth, fuller than I would have admitted.

I thought back to Bykovsky and the bus urination tradition. It seemed appropriate to carry on that ritual, to mark my territory, as it were. I carefully unzipped my flight suit and undid my connections, my tubing; I got off the bus, nonchalantly carrying my golden payload. Then I knelt by the front tire and emptied my external bladder, exactly where the hapless Bykovsky had done so just a few short hours before. And I stood and gave a little squirt from the internal one, just to be safe.

Duplicitous? Presumptuous? Bykovsky would have done the same. Everyone would have done the same.

And yet...

"What is he doing, that little Jew?" With my back to the base of the pad I hadn't seen Sergei Pavlovich, who had apparently just come down the elevator the engineer was waiting to re-ascend. He said it not to me, but to Kamanin, who was at his elbow; he said it just loudly enough that I could hear it over the various pumps and generators. I know that's what he said.

Quickly I stuffed the empty urine bag back in my suit: no time to reconnect the tubing. And no time to shake the last drops from my member. I zipped up and turned, studiously attempting to appear casual.

They walked up to me. "What's going on?" Kamanin asked.

From somewhere—the unsecured bag in my flight suit, or my unshaken penis—I could feel a few wayward drops of urine seeping into my long underwear. "Just stretching my legs, sir."

Skeptical looks from both men. Eyes darting down to the fresh wet stain on the bus tire. "Stretching your legs," Sergei Pavlovich said. Stern face, distorted jaw—broken in the 30s on his trip to the camps. No kindness in those eyes today.

"I was told I needed to be ready to go." Modified honesty: perhaps the wisest policy.

"We'll see. Get back on the bus."

I did as I was told. What choice did I have?

The wait dragged on. Now every thought was darkened, filtered by too many layers of emotions: the thrill of having been selected to train for the mission, the crushing decision from the State Commission, the sunburst of hope that I would in fact fly after all, the dark realization that perhaps I'd messed that up, too. I drew the curtains, closed myself off from the scene.

It was to be a joint flight; they were going to launch East-6 in a couple days with Tereshkova on board, and that would be the end of the program. Every flight a record, even East-5. Rockets mass-produced like sausages, triumphs rolling off the assembly line one after another, Taylorism plus Leninism equaling a glorious series of firsts. And I was part of that, right? All the training—violent spins in the centrifuge, forced isolation in the chamber, practice parachute jumps in the SK-1, hours on my back responding to lights and throwing switches—it seemed certain it would lead to something! But surely Bykovsky was thinking the same thing.

Even as the bus started filling back up, I held on to a sliver of hope. Surely they would not tell a man he was flying and then not launch him?

The lurch of the bus as it pulled away from the launch pad felt like a knife to the heart.

The curtains were still closed. I was looking at nothing. Angry and oblivious. Nothing was as real as my thoughts.

The bus ride was shorter than expected, far shorter than the trip out: just a few minutes. And I realized with horror that we had pulled up to the viewing stand. I would have to watch my humiliation with a smile.

The others filed off, but one of Kamanin's minions suggested I stay on board. The benches of the reviewing stand were weather-worn wood, rough and splintered from the harsh steppe weather; there was no point risking a puncture in my flight suit. Best to protect it, he said.

My thoughts were at war. Protect it...for what? And yet: perhaps it was best to be left alone at a time like this. "Very well."

"Let me open these curtains for you, at least."

"Thank you."

It was a clear view across two kilometers of empty steppe to the solitary rocket. I would be able to see everything. No thank you.

I waited until Kamanin's toady got off the bus before closing the curtains again. I did not wish for disaster—I am better than that, at least—but I did not wish for anything. I was twenty-eight years old; all the things I was waiting for—surprised looks of recognition from strangers on the street, trips to the special stores with my wife, knowledge that my name was on the glorious lists—would have to wait. Anonymity—for how much longer? Had I known how many years and humiliations were to follow, would I have left the program?

The rumbling of the rocket jarred loose so many emotions. My insides collapsing, a shell remaining. I did not look through the curtains. Not even a peek.

Bykovsky, of course, flew safely. Everyone knew he would fly safely, most of all me. His bright accomplishment was eclipsed in the mind of popular memory by Tereshkova, the first woman in space. And he was nice and gracious about it afterwards, which of course made it all the worse. But he still holds the record for the longest solo flight: five days. A record that will never be broken: no one flies solo any more. A record that would have been mine, but for a decision I was not privy to, made in a small room next to a capsule atop a launch pad.

This was the story I told myself for years, a story magnified by subsequent humiliations.

And yet its meaning has been reversed by the accident. Everything now means something new, since the accident.

•••

The next launch was not until Sunrise-1, a year and a half later. Did I really think I was going to fly on it?

It is difficult now to reconstruct my thoughts, sandwiched as they are between my initial bitter humiliations and my subsequent bitter triumphs. But I think I thought it was a logical certainty—when you were a backup, you were a prime next time; that's always how it worked—while trying to ignore the nagging irrational voices telling me it would never happen that way for me.

I do remember taking Tamara and Andrei on a train trip to central Moscow in early June of 1964, after I'd been picked, but before I was supposed to tell anyone. The training schedule would be picking back up soon; I wanted them to at least have some pleasant memories in case anything happened on the mission; I wanted them to know I'd chosen to spend time with them. (There are others whose passing would doubtless summon tales of drunken debauchery! I always imagine girlfriends and conquests whose identities and existence have been protected like state secrets coming out afterwards to tell their sordid tales—or, God forbid, showing up at funerals. Then again, it hadn't happened with Yuri.)

The train alone seemed enough for my son: to wait on the platform, fidgeting with anticipation, while my wife and I periodically reminded him to stay away from the edge; then to watch the electric beast pull up and open its doors; then to climb onboard and watch the scenery roll by. "Turn around! Sit on the seat!" I kept telling him, but his eager eyes and youthful curiosity kept pulling him up and around so he was kneeling on the seat and facing the windows, until finally Tamara said, "Relax!"

"He can't," I told her, exasperated. "He doesn't know how to behave."

"I'm talking to you! This is as exciting for him as going up there would be for you."

Going up there. She said it aloud, on a train. I scanned the other passengers: a handful of housewives and a vodka-soaked veteran. None of them seemed to notice.

"Let him enjoy it," she went on. "Let's let someone in the family have a fun trip."

I thought about telling her then, telling her I'd been picked: the flight that would end all fights. She was, after all, well on her way to a doctorate in metallurgy; in those years it was still an open question as to who was the more accomplished spouse. But after East-5 I was taking nothing for granted. So I stewed in silence for a few minutes before allowing myself to enjoy Andrei enjoying the ride: watching trees and apartment buildings with wide eyes, all of it fascinating and new. (Truly for a six-year-old, a suburban train ride is as exciting as a trip to space! And perhaps more so, for you at least know that the people in charge of the selection process put you there because they love you.)

By the time we transferred to the Metro, we were holding hands and enjoying each other's company. When we got off the subway I held Andrei's a little tighter, eager to keep him from being swept away in the jostling currents of commuters, but I also tried to let him admire the arcing concrete vault ceilings of the station as we made our way up to the wide busy streets. And soon we were strolling down the Alexander Gardens, basking in the summer sun as Andrei marveled at the massive Kremlin wall.

"If you're good, maybe I can ask and they'll let us inside," I told him, and he looked up at me with all the love a son has to give.

Meanwhile my wife conversed with me in the secret silent language of parents. *They let everyone inside*, her narrowing eyes seemed to say, to which my smiling ones told her: *He doesn't need to know that!*

At the Kutafya Tower I whispered in the ear of one of the guards; he nodded and gave Andrei a stern look: "Are you going to be a good boy if I let you in?"

Andrei drew himself up straight. "Yes, sir!"

"He was misbehaving on the train a little," I pointed out, and Tamara elbowed me in the ribs.

Even the guard gave me a look. "A train ride is very exciting for a young boy. But we do have to behave, especially in here." He bent down to look directly in Andrei's eyes. "There is a very big bell in there, and another little boy broke it. Just last week. And he got in a lot of trouble. You don't want to get in trouble in here. Trust me."

Andrei's eyes widened in fear; the guard stood and gave us a nod in the secret silent language of an accomplished parental accomplice, sending us on our way.

We strolled along the bridge that leads up to Troitskaya Tower; despite the guard's admonishment, Andrei didn't make it halfway up the ramp before bolting over to the side to peer through the red brick crenellations at the gardens below; I tensed, getting ready to bark an order lest he fall to his death, but Tamara belayed it with a silent hand on my arm, and a nod of the head. "Look at the tower, Andrei! Isn't that magnificent?"

Her subtle approach worked; Andrei's attention shifted from the deadly drop to the looming brick tower. But now he ran ahead, towards the tunnel and the Kremlin grounds, and inside he headed left towards the Arsenal, which I knew was off-limits.

"OK, now you have to get him," I said, and she glared: the secret silent language of parents who are not going to be sleeping together for quite some time. But she trotted ahead, and I followed, and as we got close I heard her say, "Look at that big new building," in an attempt to turn him towards the Palace of Congresses. But the sterile concrete and glass held no allure, and he kept walking towards the restricted area.

"Andrei, we're inside the fortress now," I said. "I heard there is a very big cannon up ahead, around the corner! Let's go look at it!"

"Borrowing my tactics," Tamara said.

"What do boys like? Boys like forts and cannons. You study so much, you should know these things."

"Such a great trip this is turning out to be."

"I'm just saying, you've got to know what people want, to motivate them."

"Oh, I know." A smirk. "Good luck getting lucky any time soon."

And I had to wonder: at what price victory? The way things were going, it would be a long time indeed before we slept together again.

But my plan backfired in other ways, too. Andrei held hands with us for a bit, but as we rounded the corner he saw the bronze snout of the massive cannon and took off running, faster than before.

"Brilliant plan!" Tamara said. "Boys like cannons! Now you have to go get him."

Reluctantly I trotted ahead, calling out, "Andrei! Remember what the guard said!" and jogging faster when that didn't slow him; I realized to my horror that he was going to dart through the clusters of visitors and duck under the chains that surrounded the cannon.

I pushed my way through the tittering tourists, catching snippets of commentary: "What kind of parent allows such a thing?" and "That kid's got eggs the size of those cannonballs!" And when I made it up to the chains I saw with a strange mix of horror and pride that he had placed his arms around one of the massive spheres—each one as big as him—and was trying to load the cannon.

"Andrei!" I grabbed him up, pulled him back over the chains, and scanned the scene for approaching guards muttering the inevitable questions: *Who is that man?* And: *Where does he work?*

But: no official trouble. To my son I spoke again: "You're going to hurt yourself."

"I'm pretty sure the balls are welded together," Tamara said as she came up behind me.

"I'm sure they are too, but I don't want him to hurt himself trying to move them." The bystanders were still eyeing us, enjoying our argument.

"Did the cannon kill a lot of fascists?" Andrei asked as I set him down.

"No, it was built long before the war. It's never been used."

"Are they keeping it to use against the Americans?"

I chuckled. "No. This cannon is never going to be used."

"I can think of another cannon that's never going to be used," Tamara said, in the tone of someone who wants to humiliate a spouse in public.

"Well you would know." There were chuckles from the tourists closest to me, and a flooding shame: they heard, and understood.

We dragged Andrei off to Tsar Bell, very much against his will; I held on tightly, lest he jump the chains and climb inside the bell through the gap made by the crack.

But he just stood there, slack-jawed. At last he asked: "What happened to the little boy?"

"The little boy?" Tamara asked.

"The guard said a little boy broke the bell. Is he still in trouble?"

"That was just a story," Tamara said, and I glared at her. She went on. "The bell was broken hundreds of years ago. They dug a hole in the ground to cast it, a massive pit. You see how big the bell is? That's how big the pit was."

Andrei was rapt.

"Then they had to take the bell out of the hole while it was cooling. It was a long process and it took many months. And at last they raised it out of the hole, and it was almost done cooling, but there was a big fire. And they threw water on the bell when they were fighting the fire, and it cracked, and it fell back in the pit. It was in the pit for one hundred years."

A gasp from our little boy. "How did they get it back out? Did Comrade Lenin do it?"

"No, it was before Comrade Lenin. It was a French architect."

"It wasn't a Soviet?"

"No, the Soviet Union didn't exist yet."

"Wow." He studied again the giant bell. "Why doesn't the Soviet Union fix it?"

"The Soviet Union can't do everything," Tamara said.

"Just about everything," I added, eyes on the strangers all around.

We strolled around the grounds some more, but the day was getting warmer; we decided to visit the State Historical

Museum. It was a long bit of walking, and we stopped to buy some bread from a vendor's cart outside.

"You had to tell him the truth about the bell?" I asked as we ate.

She gave a look: leave it alone.

I pressed on: "It was a useful story."

"Our country is full of useful stories. God save us from useful stories. They told you before East-5 there was a chance you'd go up. I'm sure that was a useful story."

I thought about telling her then about the new mission. I held back, and stewed.

Inside we ambled through the dark cool galleries, with Andrei studying dioramas of Neanderthals and Romanovs while my wife and I hung back. Near the end of the exhibit there was a final display, a mannequin in an orange flight suit. An SK-1, just like Yuri had worn. Just like I had worn. Indeed I couldn't help wondering if it *was* the same exact one, if they'd donated it at the end of the program. I eyed the stitching, looking for familiar patterns: Was it the same one?

"This is an exhibit about cosmonauts," Tamara said.

"I'm well aware of that." There was a placard about the flights, and the famous names: Gagarin and Titov and Nikolayev and Popovich and Tereshkova. And, of course: Bykovsky. "Believe me, I'm well aware."

"I was telling Andrei."

"What's a cosmonaut?"

"A cosmonaut is a special pilot who flies in outer space. Out where the stars and planets are."

"Papa." Andrei was looking up at me with great love. "You're a pilot. You should be a cosmonaut."

I braced myself for some crack from Tamara. Instead she looked at me, eyes unexpectedly warm, and said: "Your father will make an excellent cosmonaut someday."

Oh, the swelling of my heart! So much gratitude in that moment. What marriage is not, in the end, fed and nourished by the unexpected, by those small moments of grace that come when you're sure you're going to get the opposite entirely? I smiled, the unspoken language of spouses that says: all is forgiven.

Of course it did not last.

"Are they going to make a monument?" Andrei asked. "When Papa's a cosmonaut?"

"Perhaps," Tamara said, then started chuckling.

"What is it?"

"No, I can't..." She straightened her face, on guard against her mood. But more giggles escaped.

"Come on," I said.

She gave a secret look: I hope I won't get in trouble for what I'm about to say.

"Say it."

"All right. I was thinking about that old joke. What Voltaire said: how the most famous things in the Kremlin were a cannon that has never been fired, and a bell that has never been rung. So you'll fit in...a cosmonaut that has never flown!"

I chuckled, shook my head. My mood was still better than it had been: bread in my stomach, warmth in my heart. Plus the knowledge, held close like a cigarette in the wind, held close like my faith: they had picked me.

And yet still that thought, anxiety or prophecy: but it isn't going to happen.

We ambled back out into the bright summer day, strolled down Red Square, squeezed into the crowd to watch the smart-stepping guards at Lenin's mausoleum. Then: across to the Main Universal Store, the long white edifice almost as imposing as the Kremlin Wall opposite.

Inside: the familiar arcing iron-and-glass roofs over the creamy marble galleries. Crowds milling about on the first floor. We sized up one lengthy queue.

"What are you waiting for?" Tamara asked the man in front of us.

"In truth I don't know," he smiled. "With a line this long it has to be good, right?"

"What if you get up there and it's something you don't want?"

"Better I get it than someone else."

I nodded towards another queue, mostly female. "That one's moving faster. And there might be something I can get you."

We made our way to the front; the women were trying on headscarves while an old woman with an abacus totaled up their purchases.

"Ugh." Tamara eyed herself in the mirror as she tried on a scarf. "I look like a peasant."

"You're a most beautiful peasant." I kissed her cheek.

"Tereshkova told me a story. Gagarin took her and the other women on a shopping trip last year. Some special store on the second floor. He told them: 'You need better dresses than what you've got, my little tarts.'"

"That sounds like Yuri."

"My point is: the store. You can't get us in up there, can you?"

"Maybe after I fly."

A disappointed look.

"Trust me, I'm more eager than you." Then, against my better judgment, and in a definitive tone: "I promise, it will be soon."

Her eyes lit up. "How soon?"

"I shouldn't..."

"How soon?" An insistent smile.

"October." The cursed fateful prophecy: I regretted it as soon as it left my mouth.

"That's fantastic!"

"Yes. Fantastic."

"Seriously, I am very happy for you."

"And for the special store…"

"Not just that!" She kissed me, leaned against me, her warmth and scent summoning feelings, and more. She whispered in my ear: things I cannot share.

Home we went, lifted by hope.

Usually in the city there is a strange sadness I feel, looking at random apartment buildings, wondering what life is like inside. Whether this one offers a view of a national park forest at sunrise, or the Moscow River by moonlight; whether the occupants spend their Friday nights drinking around the dinner table, or listening to the radio, or reading on the sofa, or making passionate love; knowing I will never know. I had felt this longing on the morning train. But on the return, I caught myself thinking: perhaps I won't be anonymous, the next time I pass this way; perhaps they'll be out on their balconies for me.

Were those my only thoughts? No. Like most people, my mind flew from one topic to the next without stopping to rest. In truth I also told God in the silence of my heart that I was willing to fly, just to fly. Just so all the years of training would mean something. So I could be who I believed I was meant to be.

I did not stop Andrei from looking around on the way home; I caught myself thinking of the way he'd looked at me in the museum, the way he'd looked at me even after all the earlier unpleasantness. What had I done to deserve that? Me just being myself—that seemed enough for him.

I also caught Tamara looking at me with a smile. So many things unfinished...

Her good mood lasted all the way home, and then some. I do not want to get into all the details, but there is a strong chance our daughter was conceived that night.

•••

On Monday I was back at it, energized. And so, too, in the following months of centrifuges and simulations. There was no parachute training this time, for there were to be three of us crammed into that polished metal sphere, no bigger than East-1; there was no room for ejection seats, no way to escape if, say, the spacecraft's parachute failed on descent. There wasn't even any room for pressure suits; mass was at a premium, and we were to fly in light flight suits. But I didn't mind, because I thought there was an understanding: we were the prime crew. When the engineers had ideas, I was the one they sought out for feedback or permission. It was quite an exciting feeling, to be chosen! And despite the circuslike atmosphere—this feeling we were doing increasingly desperate tricks, and with no safety nets—we would have eagerly flown.

Still I started to feel like it wouldn't happen, even as we went through the motions and the months fell apart into weeks and the weeks dwindled into days.

The day before they flew us to the firing range, we went to the opening ceremonies for the Monument to the Conquerors of Space; we stood there under the massive arcing titanium obelisk in the chill October air and watched as Gagarin made his speech; we traded hesitant but excited glances. The monument looked like an angled exhaust plume trailing a smooth stylized rocket that was climbing to the heavens; on the sides of the base were friezes, relief sculptures of the many people responsible: engineers and technicians and workers, following the Party's leaders. Faces in the crowd, and above them, a triumph. What would it feel like, to finally be the one they looked up to? Still there was that other feeling, too.

Then: the long flight to Tyura-Tam. Final preparations, but now, whispered speculations. Were all my fears turning real? Sure enough, when the State Commission met just three short days before the flight, it was decided: we were no longer the prime crew.

Apparently no one had known during the crew selection process that Katys's father had been shot during the Great Purge. And while no one—except perhaps Kamanin—was still trying to justify the Purge, neither did anyone want to call attention to it.

As for me: Korolev would not look me in the eyes after the State Commission met.

Kamanin did not offer details. Just a clapped hand on the shoulder and a clear, definitive, "I'm sorry, Boris." He at least had the decency to do that.

Another decision I hadn't been privy to, in a room to which I hadn't been admitted.

The mood changed instantly, or so it seemed. No longer were the engineers seeking out my counsel on this setting or that; no longer were they waiting tentatively for the previous person to have their say, then rushing up to ask me for my input on their particular problem. Now instead of starting, conversations stopped when I walked into the room, replaced by furtive glances.

I, too, had questions: If Katys was the problem, why did they not just swap him out? Who had decided that I, too, would not fly? Would I ever know the names of my enemies?

For Yegorov, who had trained with us, remained on the prime crew, slated to fly with Komarov and Feoktistov now. Was it him? Was he the enemy? His father was in the Politburo, so it was certainly a possibility. Had he said something to Korolev? To Kamanin? I knew I would never know for sure.

We still suited up, in the comfortable blue flight suits now; we suited up but knew we would not fly. I knew. It was like East-5, but the little things were now slightly different—two transfer busses, for instance; one happy, one sad. Two others to share my misery. At the launch pad the prime crew laughed and joked, but mostly amongst themselves; we replied with pinched smiles. Yegorov in particular would not look at me.

Again, watching from the stands. The short bus ride was less of a disappointment this time, less of a surprise. And the flight suits were much more comfortable than the bulky SK-1. Still, bitterness: my enemies had won, again.

There was a rumor, told to me not by someone who had been in the room, but by someone who had spoken with someone who had, or someone who had spoken with *that* someone. According to the rumor, Sergei Pavlovich Korolev himself had said: "That little Jew will never fly, so long as I'm alive."

Tamara, needless to say, was furious. I could not speak to her about it, other than to let her know it had happened. For months I could not speak to her about it.

And Andrei still loved me, in spite of it all.

●●●

That next summer I found myself waiting on the train platform with Andrei, just the two of us this time. Still unflown and unknown.

Sunrise-1 had flown successfully, only to be eclipsed in turn by Sunrise-2. Blondie—Leonov—was still touring the world, still being toasted for his fragile triumph. It had been so lucky, so nearly a disaster, that some of us were saying even then that he'd used up all the good fortune for the rest of us, that things were bound to come down sooner or later. Still, I was on the slate again for Sunrise-3, and it seemed wise to do something enjoyable with my family before the long (and hopefully fruitful, this time) days of training. But Tatyana had just been born, and with Tamara I was always in the wrong, especially that year—either wrong for not helping out, or wrong for getting in the way when I tried. So on this trip it was just Andrei and I.

He stood there like a good little boy, arms down and possibly a little stiff at his side, avoiding the edge of the platform as if on an invisible leash. Eyes darting down the empty rails, past the indecipherable signals, then back up to look for mine. And when the train at last appeared he waited patiently as it rolled to its hissing and rattling stop; he climbed on board and looked around at the smattering of commuters, then up to me for approval. "You can sit by the window!" I said.

I was eager not just to have a good time, but to remember it well; we hadn't taken pictures on our previous family outing, but this time I had a small camera on a leather strap around my neck, and darkroom chemicals waiting at home. I wanted to capture that look on his face, the look of pure excitement when the train started moving. But when he took his seat he sat up straight, hands flat against his thighs, head forward. It did not look like it would make for a good photograph, but I took one anyway before taking my seat.

"It's nice to take a day together, huh? Just us men?" Our family had felt a little uneven before Tatyana, but now with the four of us there were multiple symmetries and redundancies, and it pleased the engineer in me: two males, two females; two adults, two children; two male-female pairs, two same-sex pairs.

He said nothing. Eyes straight ahead, then darting up.

"You can turn and look out the window if you'd like! Just don't get your feet on the seat."

He turned, somewhat stiffly; he watched the countryside as the train accelerated down the rails; I took another picture. But there was something mechanical about all of it.

I took out a paperback and read it in fits and starts while the train made its scheduled stops. Finally I could take it no more. "All right, what's wrong?"

But he said nothing.

"You can talk to me, Andrei."

Quiet muttered words: "I don't want to go back to the Kremlin."

"We didn't get any pictures last year! The big cannon, the big bell..."

"I want to go somewhere new." Quiet, but full of determination.

"We're already on the train, Andrei." There was, a few seats away, an ancient grandmotherly woman with a deeply lined face; I imagined her judging me for having such an insolent child.

Again: "I want to go somewhere new."

Exasperation: "We're already on the train."

And now the old woman spoke. "There's a new monument to the cosmonauts. Near the trade show place."

"Really?" I answered in the most sarcastic tone possible. How could I forget the bitter fall air, how small I'd felt in the shadow of that monument?

"It's made of some special metal that they use in the spaceships." Warm but not wise—or to be fair, just not psychic.

"Well I'll have to check it out!"

And the old bat took this as encouragement! "It should be an inspiring place for a little boy...perhaps he'll grow up to be a cosmonaut! We parents always realize at some point that we've missed these opportunities, but children are full of potential!"

"Indeed." The senile old hag! How dare she.

Then: "You know, this train went past Star City. I think the one who did the spacewalk lives there. Leonov."

"I heard that as well." I turned my back on her with exaggerated motions, hoping she'd get the hint.

But it was too late. "Papa. We should go to the cosmonaut memorial."

"You're already on the way!" The old woman didn't realize how unhelpful she was being.

"Can we go, Papa?" The light in those eyes as he looked up at me—what father could say no?

But I tried. "We're already on the train."

"You can go!" the woman said. "You just have to get off and take the bus!"

"It's too late for that," said a younger man across the aisle. "You need the Metro now."

"No, the bus," the old woman said as the train rolled to a stop. "You just have to get off here."

I made it a point to stay on, even though I knew Andrei's eyes would eventually bore holes in my parental armor, straight through to my conscience.

And so after a somewhat roundabout journey, we found ourselves at VDNKh. Barrel-vaulted tunnels, jostling crowds, broken escalators: we slogged in an endless line up, up, up from the belly of the impossibly deep station to the bright day. A wearying journey as punishment for my many failings.

Then, more punishment: the angled titanium monument, rippled and shining, looking even more spectacular than it had on that drab October day. The stylized exhaust plume summoning the eyes skyward to the smooth perfect rocket, gleaming gloriously in the sunlight. Headed to space with no involvement on my part, while I watched from a close distance.

Andrei stood there, mouth agape, taking it all in—looking happier than he'd been all day. "Wow!" he said over and over, darting about to see it from different angles. Listlessly I pointed out the friezes on the side, scientists and pioneers looking forward to the glorious future under Lenin's wise eyes and outstretched arm; I squatted and pointed out the related statue of Tsiolkovsky, the visionary, and read aloud the quotation on the pedestal, the one about our efforts being rewarded, about overcoming lawlessness and forging fiery wings. And here—here, of course!—he wanted me to take pictures. So I did, squatting low to capture his short body and the big monument, trying to enjoy his enjoyment.

Then at last I stood and stretched, looking off down the promenade. "You know, there is more to see here than just the monument."

"But I like the monument." Still he was staring up at it in awe.

"You'll like the exhibition grounds." I gestured towards the promenades leading to the exhibition center. "There are fountains. Pavilions. A giant arch…"

Still he stood, transfixed.

"Perhaps the little boy would like to see a spacecraft." An older woman, a passerby. The woman from the train? No, impossible!

Still, too late: "A spacecraft?"

"Yes, in one of the pavilions there's a spacecraft on display. Just like East-1." She stretched her arm out like Lenin, towards a bitter past that still felt like a glorious future for everyone but me. "Over that way."

And now the boy, who had been rooted in place, was practically dragging me away. We passed under the magnificent white-and-gold entrance archway and barely gave it a glance; we did not linger to look at the fountains and their glorious golden statues; we stopped tourist after tourist until we finally got directions to the proper building.

Inside, at the end of a long arched gallery of glass and steel— a large reverent space, almost like a church—stood the spacecraft, perched high on a pylon at a dramatic angle. The familiar gleaming metal sphere bristling with antennae, atop

151

a tan metal canister adorned with tanks and fittings and a rocket nozzle in the back, all of it perfect and new. Behind it: an artistic rendition of a space backdrop. Blue waning crescent moon, a smattering of stars, blue arcs of atmosphere, just like I'd heard about. Blue, blue, blue.

"Wow." Andrei stood there transfixed, perhaps imagining himself at the controls. Which, to be fair, I was doing, too.

Around us tourists ambled, read plaques, posed for pictures. A sandy-haired man about my age knelt with his arm around a skeptical-eyed son armed with a red toy Kalashnikov. "Can you believe it? This is what Gagarin flew in space! This same exact spacecraft! That part that looks like a can, that's where he lived, in space! And when it was time to come home he fired the rocket and flew it back down, and now it's here in..."

Finally I had enough. "This wasn't in space."

"I think it was! I was just telling him..." A nod towards his son. "The plaque says this is the East spacecraft. And that's the one Gagarin flew on..."

"No. This is an engineering display model. It never flew. And the cosmonaut doesn't go in the can part. That's the equipment module. They discard it and it burns up in the atmosphere. The cosmonaut stays in the ball part; that's the only part that comes back. And it's charred afterwards."

"Are you sure?" (The man smiled and gave a nod towards the little boy, and...was that a wink? I remember thinking maybe it wasn't really his son; maybe he was a sex pervert.) "I was just telling him..."

A confident smile. "I'm pretty sure."

Then I looked over and Andrei was gone.

I scanned the milling tourists, the eager innocent faces; I darted around imagining I'd spot some other pervert trying to drag Andrei off to God knows what fate. I imagined what would happen if I didn't catch him, if I had to report it all to the police. *Bring him back in one piece*, Tamara had said that morning, and I'd responded sarcastically: *Oh! You want me to take care of our only son, and not lose him! I hadn't considered that!* And now I could picture the frustrated hours waiting at the police station, the tongue-tied telephone call, the tongue-lashing...

What could I do? I had to do something. I paced the length of the gallery, forward and back, my pulse and my steps quickening, camera thudding against my chest. How could I be so oblivious? Back where I started I spun around, frantic. Stupid, stupid, stupid!

There. There he was, studying a plaque beneath the spaceship, in the shadow of another man.

"Andrei!"

He startled a little when he looked up and realized the other man was not his father; he looked at me with fear as I trotted up.

I grabbed him by the shoulders, placed a finger under his chin, lifted it so his eyes would look into mine. "What did I say about behaving? You mustn't wander off in crowded places!"

His eyes welled, watered, burst. "I was just trying to learn about the spacecraft."

"I was…" (Seeing those tears gave me pause. Dear God, what was I doing?) "I'm sorry, I…I just don't want anything to happen to you."

For the next half hour I pointed out various features on the spacecraft and what they did; I explained why the engineers had made their various choices. I knelt and pointed to this antenna and that rocket motor, explained about missile stages and launch shrouds, told stories about various flights: who messed up, who got sick. I stayed down by his side until my muscles burned and ached. He asked for pictures and I took them; he made me ask a stranger to take a picture of us together beneath the spacecraft. Only when he asked about the bathroom did we finally walk away.

Afterwards we headed outside, taking time now to gaze at the fountains, to scan the faces in the summer crowds. We stopped at a vendor cart and bought rolls of bread for a few kopecks, then sat down to relax and snack.

"Well it certainly has been a memorable trip," I told him. "I hope you've been enjoying it."

"Can I have a balloon?"

"A balloon?"

"I saw some boys with balloons. The kind that float."

"Helium balloons."

"Yes. Over there." He nodded towards two young boys with balloon strings clenched in their small fists.

I imagined how long he'd have one before he'd slip up and let it go; I imagined the balloon drifting up into the summer sky, getting sucked into the engine of a jetliner, causing a flaming catastrophe. Then again: perhaps it was time to teach him about personal responsibility. "We can certainly look into getting you a balloon."

"A blue one." Again the quiet determination.

"All right, little man. I'll make it my mission."

We brushed the crumbs from our laps and set out to find the balloon vendor. It seemed a simple case of propagation and diffusion; I scanned the ambling tourists for balloons, and kept dragging Andrei down the promenade looking for higher concentrations of them until I found the apparent source, a cluster anchored to a vendor cart that was topped with a parasol.

"Can I get this young man a blue balloon?" I asked as I walked up. The vendor was an old woman in a shawl; she looked familiar. Her cart was covered with toys: squeaky rabbits, inflatable beach balls, a red-and-yellow airplane. I supposed I was getting off easy...

"Oh! They have a spaceman!" Andrei squealed with delight. And sure enough, beneath the sun umbrella was an orange toy cosmonaut, dangling from its string like Leonov at the end of his umbilical cord.

"Well, there are a few other options. And if you get a toy, no balloon."

"It sounds like the boy would really like a spaceman." The vendor's eyes twinkled mischievously.

A fist of anger or angst clenched around my heart: this really was too much. But unfortunately I caught the expectant hopeful look in my son's eyes, and I had to choke down my pride. "How much?"

"Two rubles."

A sting. But I couldn't lie; I did have it. And so as my son looked on with delight I pulled out my wallet and bought a toy version of my rival, Korolev's new favorite son.

On the train home, Andrei was no longer the rigid boy of morning; he snuggled under my arm and fell asleep on my chest to the train's soothing rhythms. I awkwardly took the camera off and gave it to the stranger across the aisle so he could take a picture of me and my slumbering boy. It was the last picture on the roll, so I carefully rewound the film with my free hand, making sure it was back in the canister so I wouldn't open it and expose the film. I even removed the roll and pocketed it one-handed, so as to not disturb my sleeping boy. When I finally had to wake him at our station, he was so groggy and disoriented that he forgot about the orange copy of Alexei Leonov on the seat next to him. I thought about ushering him off the train before he remembered it—surely a necessary lesson, to keep track of your possessions on the train!—but my conscience was now attached to this toy by invisible strings, and I picked it up as we departed.

•••

In the days and weeks to come, the training schedule did pick up, but more slowly than expected. It was evident to all that no one on Sunrise-3 would be spacewalking, but I did at least think I'd fly. For sure I thought I would fly. So when I came home late on training nights and saw the orange cosmonaut dangling from his string—we had secured him to the ceiling with a hook; Andrei wanted to see him at all times—I was eventually not perturbed. I figured perhaps next year we'd have a model of the Sunrise up there on a string, because by then I'd have done something impressive myself.

But I did not know what.

At first there was talk of gravity experiments, swinging the spaceship around on a tether. Then in December Gemini 7 went to space and stayed for two whole weeks. And in January Korolev went to the hospital and stayed for two whole months. There was talk of changing our mission to one of simple duration, just to get the record back from the Americans. But with Korolev out, no one was confident in pushing the Sunrise spacecraft so far past its design parameters; Mishin arranged a test flight to verify the spacecraft's capabilities, and the dogs came back in very poor condition indeed. The new goal—an eighteen-day mission—seemed quite out of reach. Our launch was pushed back from March to April to May; we still went through the motions of training, but half-heartedly. Korolev came back from the hospital and started questioning things; I started again to feel some displeasure when I noticed Leonov hanging from his string in my son's room, untouchable.

Then: Sunrise-3 was canceled.

It was canceled ten days before the flight, with the rocket already on the launch pad. We were still training in Star City, so I did not suffer again the indignity of seeing it and knowing I wouldn't be riding it. That seemed like a slight improvement in the data trend.

But it was hard to find anything else positive, with the program in such disarray. Mishin had been dithering too much, and making bad decisions when he did commit to something; I was quite sure Korolev had seen where things were headed and had emerged from the hospital purely out of spite, to get things back on course.

And I do have to admit, canceling Sunrise-3 might have been right. Korolev saw no need to launch a dead-end design just to steal one more record from the Americans; he marshalled his resources and redirected our efforts towards launching the Union; he even made his peace with the hated Glushko so we could be on a good footing as we got started in earnest towards the moon.

Then: collapse. Another trip to the hospital for Korolev. Stomach cancer: discovered in January but not disclosed to us. This time he did not return.

I tried to breathe. I tried to relax. I tried to wait my turn.

$$\bullet \bullet \bullet$$

The morning of the Union-2 launch, everyone at the firing range kept clapping me on the back and telling me: it's your lucky day at last.

I smiled back tentatively; amidst the handful of familiar faces were others I'd probably last seen at East-5, all perceptibly older: wrinkles around eyes, reading glasses, gray hair at temples. I did not know their names, but they seemed happy for me, and there was something heart-warming in that.

Still I did not take the launch for granted. I had been through this too many times to take anything for granted. My enemies were still out there.

Union-1, the rendezvous craft, had launched yesterday: Old Man Beregovoy flying solo, for the moment. I had Shatalov and Yeliseyev with me, for the moment. We rode together in the transfer bus—still the same bus, spotted now with rust!—and they chatted and joked. But I was distant; unlike them, I had ridden the bus before. What was for them the start of a new adventure was for me a reminder of bitter humiliations. We still had a reserve crew; they were still suited up as well. They had been eyeing us all morning, giving little nods as if to acknowledge the fact that yes, they were ready too, and they'd take our seats in a heartbeat. It would only take a decision in some other room, a decision I was not privy to.

At the launch pad, my crew and I ascended together in the elevator. This at least was new; I had watched the elevator's rise and fall from the transfer bus on East-5, and again on Sunrise-1.

The technician in the orbital module guided us down through the hatch so we could take our seats: knees bent, feet close together, bodies arrayed outwards like a fan. Nothing we hadn't done in training. Then he closed the hatch, and we were alone for the remaining minutes before launch, running tests and making banal chatter. The expected notices came: ten minutes' readiness, five minutes' readiness, one minute readiness. And I pressed the expected buttons with my reaching stick. But all of it was still very easily reversible, and I knew there were those who would do so, just to spite me.

I did not know for sure that it was actually going to happen until I felt the rumble of the rocket beneath my back.

Even then I monitored the instruments carefully. At the lurch of liftoff I could see in my peripheral vision that Shatalov and Yeliseyev each raised a clenched fist in celebration, a quick and happy gesture. Premature, to my mind. We were not in orbit; we could not even see anything out the windows. An absurd thought came to mind: that it was all an elaborate hoax, that we were still on the pad and they were shaking the spacecraft mechanically...

But no, the acceleration was still pressing us downward, the rocket surging skyward, steadily pushing us into the majestic heavens. Yet another derivative of Old Number Seven, performing perfectly even though it was carrying me. Then: the jolt of staging, boosters flying away, Korolev's cross fluttering behind us, unseen.

Fairing separation, finally. Sunlight streaming through the windows. It was real.

Three minutes after launch, Control came on: "One hundred kilometers. Congratulations, you're cosmonauts now!" And Shatalov and Yeliseyev lifted their arms against the g-forces and reached across my chest to clasp their gloved hands in congratulations. Two men picked after me. Belatedly I put my hand atop theirs to join in the celebration. It had been a long time coming.

Still we were far from done. Still the rocket had to keep pushing; still there were buttons to press with my reaching stick; still there was the press of the second stage for another minute or so.

Then came the jolt as that too separated. But of course we were not yet in orbit. If the third stage failed we would fall to earth in a long arc: a shorter flight than Yuri, a spacecraft full of Shepards and Grissoms, unremarkable except for the magnitude of our failure.

I kept monitoring my kneepad checklist, kept waiting for any anomaly in the instruments. Those minutes of the third stage were, by far, the longest of the ascent.

Then at last the final shudder. The third stage falling away behind us, unseen. The solar panels snapping smoothly outward. The spacecraft set in its yaw-axis spin so it could soak up the sun like a loose lily pad turning smoothly on the surface of a pond.

Soon we were unstrapped, marveling at the view. The arc of horizon, the blurred edge of blue above it, just like the spacecraft diorama at VDNKh—finally I had seen it myself! Finally, after all these years. This thin band of air, so insignificant we had poked through it in our hollow aluminum tube: how little protection we have from the blackness! Land and sea and clouds, mottled and beautiful.

"Better than getting fucked," Yeliseyev said; I gave him a dirty look.

"Looks like it *is* your lucky day," Shatalov said to me.

A bitter smile. "I'm up here for a few more days, though."

•••

On the second day it was time to rendezvous.

We strapped in and turned on the Needle system; it executed a series of burns to bring our orbit in line with Beregovoy's. His spacecraft grew: first a distant star, then a bright metal shape, then a full ship, exotic and new, floating a few hundred meters away.

We turned off the system and flew together that way, a full orbit, enough time to unstrap and use the bathroom and eat a floating lunch during the orbital night. That was our mistake.

"That went well enough," I told Shatalov as I distributed food. "Maybe it's still my lucky day."

"Well I feel lucky," he said.

"The word is, you're both bad luck," Yeliseyev said.

"Me?" Shatalov asked.

"Your phone number ends in -13, does it not?"

"It does," he conceded.

"There was talk of that at the State Commission. Or so I'm told."

"Absurd! It's an issue for a lot of people!" Shatalov pointed out.

"Probably one percent of people," I added unnecessarily. We dug into our food, bodies arrayed at odd angles in weightless space, puffy faces unfamiliar.

"But only you, in the cosmonaut corps," Yeliseyev said. "And they launched us at 1300 hours. And today is the 13th." He nodded to me. "And you, the number of times you've been passed over…"

"It becomes a self-fulfilling prophecy," I told him. "The bad luck man. The scapegoat. People like it; it's a convenient fiction. It allows them to pretend bad fortune is something external to them, something they can keep at bay."

"The scapegoats like it, too!" Shatalov said. "It's an identity! It gives them a good story. 'Oh, poor me! Look how unlucky I am!'"

Here I bristled. "If my enemies want to stab me in the back and call me unlucky, that's their business. I told Kamanin after Sunrise-3 was canceled: 'Give me a flight! We'll see how lucky I am!' And here we are now on Union-2."

They recoiled as if my bitterness were physical blows.

"Still, one of us is the thirteenth cosmonaut," Yeliseyev said slowly.

Shatalov totted up launches and cosmonauts on his fingers: the six soloists on the East flights, three together on Sunrise-1, two on Sunrise-2, Beregovoy on Union-1: "Say, he's right!"

"We were upside-down going through the hundred-kilometer mark." He nodded to me. "The way our feet were positioned, I think it was you."

I shook my head, polished off my beef.

A grin spread across Shatalov's face. "It was a three-way tie." And to Yeliseyev: "You flew up here with him! You should want him to be lucky!"

Yeliseyev smirked. "At least for the next few hours!"

At this even I had to laugh.

Darkness ended with us flying high over a South American dawn; we strapped back in and turned on the radio to summon Beregovoy.

He was already calling. "Baikal, this is Amur. Baikal, this is Amur. Come in. Over."

"Amur, this is Baikal," I spoke. "Ready to commence docking operations. Over."

"Baikal, position your ship as instructed. Over." Gruff, obtuse.

"Time to get fucked," Yeliseyev muttered off-microphone.

I gave an ugly glance. With a quick thruster pulse I placed us in position as instructed, upside-down relative to the earth. "Amur, we are in position. Over."

"Baikal, commencing docking. One hundred meters. Over."

"Copy, one hundred meters." The sensors on the system were still showing red, though. I flipped them off, flipped them back on again.

"Baikal, fifty meters. Over."

"Copy, fifty meters." But the sensors were still red. On the periscope viewscreen I could see him drawing closer. "Amur, our sensors are red. Over."

"Baikal, it must be a glitch. Twenty meters. Over."

"Just lie there and wait for it," Yeliseyev muttered.

Still the sensors stayed red. On the screen things were getting clearer; his antennas did look strange. And then it crystallized: "*He's* upside-down." And Yeliseyev said, "Christ," but I was already calling it out: "Break off! Break off!" Radio Beregovoy said, "We're almost there," and I said: "No! Break off!" And I pulsed the thrusters and waited for: a thud, metal colliding, the hiss of decompression.

Nothing.

"Baikal, what seems to be the problem? Over." Impossibly, he sounded even more obtuse.

"Amur, you are upside-down! Over."

"Baikal, that's impossible. I reoriented. Over."

"Before lunch, or after?"

No response.

"He must have drifted," Yeliseyev muttered. "And he didn't even realize the planet was on the wrong side."

Shatalov switched us to intercom, spoke for our ears only. "I know he flew ground attack during the war. Maybe he was jealous of the fighters."

Yeliseyev and I both gave a look.

"He almost got a kill finally!" Shatalov explained. "He could have painted a silhouette of a Union on the side of his Union!"

I shook my head. "I'm not sure a ramming would count."

At last, on the radio: "Baikal, let's go again. Over."

"Fuck your mother," Yeliseyev said before we switched back to transmit. "We *are* getting fucked."

But after the maneuver we were higher, drifting a little. I nulled out the rates but the approach angle was all wrong. "Amur, we need to talk to Control through the range ships soon. We need to set up again. Over."

We busied ourselves with other tasks. Soon Control explained that yes, we had been right, and yes, we would need to set up again. There was at least the comfort of correctness; it was small, and it hurt to hold on to, but they couldn't take that away from me.

On the second try it did not go much better. The sensor lights were green intermittently; we could see him drifting in the periscope and on the monitor. Again I paused the proceedings. Again Beregovoy was upset.

"The way he's moving," Yeliseyev said, "it's like he's trying to fuck us drunk. What does he expect us to say? 'Go ahead, old man! Stick it anywhere it fits!'"

"He's got to be low on fuel at this point," Shatalov muttered. Unspoken the thought: having to return separately, having failed to get a first.

"I can hear you." Beregovoy on the radio! I realized with a start: we hadn't switched to intercom.

Yeliseyev gave a pained look. If they did make it over there, it would be an awkward ride home.

"We're going to have to talk with the coded signal signs," I told Beregovoy. Then to Shatalov: "You remember when I talked about this in training?" Because I had—I had foreseen this exact scenario.

Shatalov unstrapped. "I thought the automatic system would be sufficient. But yes, you were right."

It was almost worth it all, just to hear that. All the years of humiliation: it was almost worth it.

We explained it to Beregovoy, how we were going to make the approach, how Shatalov was going to signal using the system.

Then: the approach. On the screen his ship grew larger— smoothly this time. And at last the rough shudder: probe in drogue. Absolute relief. We had done it. I had done it.

"He should have used petroleum jelly," Yeliseyev said, after making extra sure we were on intercom only.

"You still have to spend the rest of the night with him." We still had time to do the transfer; it would cut into dinner, but at this point we were eager to get it over with.

"There was a rumor I heard," Yeliseyev said as we started unstowing the suits. "He failed his first prelaunch. Two out of five."

"And they still let him fly?" This was too much by far.

"He flew under Kamanin, during the war. Kamanin arranged for a second prelaunch."

A second prelaunch. My blood throbbed. Five years of people bending over backward to *not* give me a flight. And he fails a prelaunch and still gets up here... "Well I can believe it."

"That's not comforting," Yeliseyev said. "Not with what we're about to do!"

I smiled. "Look at it this way. You're lucky! You get to go home without the thirteenth cosmonaut!"

"But with Mr. Phone Number 13. In addition to Old Man Beregovoy. We'll see where the bad luck goes when the spacecraft separate."

"You never know," Shatalov said. "Maybe it's hiding in the transfer case."

I helped them suit up, a humorous floating mess of spacesuits and cosmonauts. Most of the laughter was from them, though. First flights, first spacewalks: it was hard to feel completely good about that. We turned on the cameras, showed the people what we were carrying over: yesterday's newspapers, with news of Beregovoy's launch for him to read, and two pieces of mail for him.

"We should have brought him reading glasses," I said once the cameras were off.

Yeliseyev laughed. "He probably does need them! The old fucker. No wonder this was a mess." He bent forward, a geriatric Beregovoy squinting at the controls. "'What does the panel say? There's no one to read it!'"

And then they were fully suited, helmets on and visors locked, floating free. A mess of umbilical cords and life support packs in the orbital module. Still they were giddy, like kids getting ready to play in the snow. I tried to be happy for them.

"Safe travels," I said as I closed the interior hatch.

I was worried about them. I should not have been worried about them.

•••

Of course, the transfer went well. And for the next few days I had what I'd missed on East-5, what Bykovsky had: a peaceful solo flight. Better, even: a newer spacecraft, more room.

I no longer wanted what Bykovsky had.

There was plenty of work to do: experiments and observations. But between tasks I found myself thinking about Shatalov and Yeliseyev, hearing again their voices on the spacewalk as they marveled at the expansive views. I was the commander, I had saved the mission; I was a success at last. And it *had* been remarkable—the first docking of two manned spacecraft. Intellectually I knew that should have been enough. And at times it was. Here and there, I was *there*, lost in the vast views: incomprehensible deserts, inviting oceans. But I wanted more.

The moon was coming. Everyone knew it, and once this mission was over it would be the biggest thing on anyone's mind. The only thing. And although in reality success is so often born of failure, and vice versa, there is that foolish perception that a track record of success is a guarantee of future success.

When I got back I would finally take advantage of that perception. Or so I thought.

Beregovoy and the others landed without incident. I was thrilled, although a small thought gnawed at my mood, like a mouse I couldn't find or kill: Where had all the bad luck gone? Perhaps they'd taken the wrong kind in the transfer case.

With their half of the mission closed and done, I knew it was all the more imperative that I do my part right. I buckled down, shook off the gnawing thoughts, focused on the work. I was up here, after all; I had made it up here at last, and not even my enemies could take that away from me. And yet it did not feel important for its own sake; it felt important because it would get me up here again on a big mission, a moon mission, perhaps the first. I had flown a rendezvous successfully. There was a glorious future coming, and I would be a part of it. As long as I finished my mission well.

When the descent started, it seemed like I had. The S5.35 fired smoothly; I felt the spacecraft settle into my back for the long minutes of the retro burn. The Gulf of Guinea was passing beneath me, and—perhaps too early—I allowed myself the luxury of fantasizing freely. Control had praised me, repeatedly! I could practically hear the whispered conversations when they turned off their microphones, or chatted on the way to the bathroom: *Perhaps we were wrong about Boris. Just think: how lucky we were to have him up there! We'll need that luck to land on the moon.*

The burn ended, exactly as expected. The pyrocartridges fired, a series of sledgehammer blows, exactly as expected. Control had sent the proper commands and the sequencer had worked properly. Or so I thought.

Outside the portholes, I could still see the solar panel's antennas.

Catastrophe.

If the antennas were still there, the solar panels were still there. If the solar panels were still there, the instrument module had failed to separate. If the instrument module had failed to separate, my heat shield was covered; I would enter wrong-end first, unprotected.

I pressed the buttons again, the buttons I had already pressed. I pressed them harder, imagining it would make a difference, imagining I had not felt what I had already felt, the pounding of the pyrocartridges firing. I pressed the buttons again, so hard my thumb flushed pink and my fingernail went white. I would not report this before I had to.

I had to.

The ionization blackout was coming up; they had to know. Surely the relay ship was still in range, down below. "Control, this is Union-2, calling emergency. We have a failure of separation of the instrument module. Over."

"Union-2, copy..." Then, realizing the seriousness. "Union-2, our telemetry is indicating the module has separated. Did you say it's still there? Over." Beneath the professionalism: disbelief.

"Control, I can still see the solar panel antennas outside my portholes. Over."

I imagined they would radio up some extra command, some emergency step that would save me. Instead: "Copy, Union-2. We are monitoring your telemetry. Good luck."

Good luck! I wanted to pound something. Now I could imagine them muting their microphones and saying to one another: *It was bound to catch up with us, sooner or later. It only figures it would happen with Boris. He's a dead man.*

Africa tumbling slowly beneath me. All those places I'd never see. I thought of Yuri: something similar had happened on his flight, and he'd still made it down. But that was a different spacecraft, a much smaller instrument module with no solar panels. He'd had a later date with Destiny.

At any rate I would not be so lucky as that. I was not Yuri; no one was. That fact was clear to all, especially me.

A faster turn of the horizon. Jerky movements. The thrusters were firing uselessly, trying harder to reorient the descent module; as far as the spacecraft knew, everything had happened properly, and it was burning large quantities of propellant to maintain that illusion. The antennas were quivering a little, but they held fast. Against the white of distant clouds I caught the first sight of the pale pink glow that would kill me.

The spacecraft stabilized—in the wrong position. A bullet with wings, hurtling forward through the thickening sky; a ground attack aircraft with crazy old Beregovoy at the controls, shooting at German tanks, laughing maniacally.

Was it getting hotter?

"Control. This is Baikal. Communications check. Over."

But they were gone. The ionization blackout: I was in it alone.

No longer weightless, I found myself pushed the wrong way—forward—with the straps pressing strangely into my shoulders. All wrong, all wrong, all wrong. Eyeballs-out gravity, nothing we had ever practiced in the rickety old centrifuge.

A mild shudder now. Sweat on my face: I *was* getting hotter.

It welled up, dampening my cheeks; backwards g-forces pulled it down the sides of my nose and to a swelling drop on the tip that dripped and drifted slowly towards the flimsy hatch that was fighting a doomed-to-lose holding action against the furnace outside.

The droplet of sweat hit the hatch. I swear I saw it sizzle. And there was more pink outside, and the antennas were fluttering violently, and then they were gone, but I knew that was not enough; if anything things were worse, for now there was less drag on the instrument compartment, less chance it would break off. Wingless now, the bullet: no way to stop it.

The spacecraft was shuddering towards its fiery violent end and the straps were pressing tighter, all wrong against my shoulders, but I could still reach my logbook. I could still reach my logbook.

The hatch was deforming. Either it would let go straight back, into my face, or hang on the hinge for a moment as the heat swirled in all at once and I met my end— incinerated like so many, but alive for it.

They could never say what had happened. Their final moments would never be real to anyone else. I had an obligation to chronicle this, to leave some memories that might survive. Someone else had to know.

The hatch was deforming; outside all was bright neon pink. And now: the scent of burning rubber. The seals were not designed for this, and soon they would stop doing what they had never been asked to do. More sweat, more sweat: a dry sauna with bitter smells. Spaceship buffeting. Beyond discomfort now: I knew I did not have much time.

Hanging upside-down in the straps, shaking from the spacecraft's death-seeking forward plunge, sweat pooling on my face and dripping and sizzling on the hatch below, I scribbled notes on the blank pages at the back of the logbook. SPACECRAFT ORIENTED FORWARD. HATCH DEFORMED AND FAILING. SEALS BURNING. IT WON'T BE LONG. DON'T LET THIS HAPPEN TO ANYONE ELSE.

Still I plunged; still the glow increased; still I sweated, hotter and hotter; still the hatch deformed and the burning smells intensified. Memories flashed: the first round of training, men turning purple and passing out in the heat chamber. My heart pumped molten lava. How could my note survive if I did not? I crammed it into the middle of the logbook. And I remembered: the rendezvous notes! I had accomplished that; that had to count for something. I tore out those pages too, stuffed them deep inside the book, crammed the book awkwardly behind my seat, as far back as I could with the bad angle and the negative gravity. But I wondered: should I have written…

An explosion outside: a propellant tank. The book shook loose from its hiding place and flew forward to land on the sizzling hatch. Oh, for fuck's sake!

But with a violent shudder the spacecraft spun around; the book hung for a split second on the handle before it flew back and hit me in the face.

The hatch had held. The instrument module had broken off. I was alive.

But for how much longer? The parachute compartments faced forward. What had happened to *those* hatches? For all I knew the main chute and the reserve were now both molten masses of plastic.

The logbook was behind and beneath me, out of reach now. But I remembered: we had a tape recorder. Could that survive? I strained my reaching stick against the now-positive g-forces; I flipped the switch to record from my headset and started to describe everything that had happened so far, so they'd know.

Outside: still the awful glow. Enough to make anyone believe hell is real. Still I could be calm; still I could face it like a man...

I stopped the tape recorder. Then I realized: I needed to say something to Tamara.

Downward I plummeted. Gravity intensifying: far more than the expected four gs. I tried to reach the panel again but my arm was too heavy and I fumbled the stick; even my wristwatch felt like a weight. The propellant was gone; the module could not steer itself to mitigate the trajectory; I was enduring a ballistic reentry.

The glow faded. The g-forces slackened. I was through the worst of it.

Outside now, the sound of high wind. Dark skies. Ten kilometers up: the drogue parachute streaked spaceward and the module jerked about.

"Control, I am under the drogue." Were they listening? A ballistic reentry: I had to be hundreds of kilometers from the designated spot.

Down, down, down. The spacecraft slowing now. Bluer skies. I had made it, so long as the main parachute deployed correctly.

The main parachute did not deploy correctly.

It came out in a twisted mass, lines turned around each other, a tight spiral. It was not going to fully inflate.

I could not believe it. After all this, I could not believe it.

Should I jettison the main and deploy the reserve? It was half the size. And for all I knew it was in worse shape.

The ground drew closer. The heat shield dropped off to expose the soft-landing rockets. Would they be sufficient for what I faced? It seemed unlikely.

And then: the parachute started untwisting. It untwisted slowly, slowly, slowly, and the horizon loomed in the portholes, and it started to catch more air, and I wondered if...

BOOM!

A truck to the back, collapsing the shock absorbers under my seat; a hockey stick to the face somehow as well.

Stillness.

This had to be the end. Dazed, I put my hand to my face. Pulled it away: blood. Pain. My front teeth, broken and loose. Nothing was firm except the ground that cradled my battered spacecraft beneath my bruised back. This was worse than what happened to Yuri on East-1. But better than his end, I had to remind myself.

Like a robotic dog I reached up and pulled the levers to release the parachute, to keep the wind from dragging my dented capsule across the barren steppe. Control trusted us enough to do that much, at least.

I did not want to go anywhere else. Not for a while.

●●●

In the hospital my family came to visit. Tamara brought the newspaper and held my hand as I read it. *Union-2, carrying first-time cosmonaut Boris Volynov, touched down successfully in the Kazakh S.S.R., two days after it joined with Union-1 in the historic first docking of two manned spacecraft.* That was all.

She kissed me on the forehead, held her hand on my shoulder. That was nice.

● ● ●

I had decided to wait this time, to only take a family excursion *after* the flight.

We waited a couple weeks, until my mouth was healed— until my false front teeth were an accepted fact of life. This time it was the four of us; this time we were headed to the circus; this time Andrei carried the camera. He snapped a few pictures on the platform as Tatyana scampered after him, in tottering pursuit of a brother who was towering to her; every time he tried to get a shot, she resolutely refused to pose, or stay in the frame; he only had a few seconds per picture before she reached an arm up, or darted up to him again.

"Don't waste film," I told him.

"She doesn't understand pictures," Tamara echoed. "She only wants to play with her big brother."

"We're going to take a family picture," I added. "Once we get down there."

Soon enough we were down there, at the yellow brick building on Tsvetnoy, but the show was about to start, so we rushed inside without taking pictures. Inside we handed our tickets to the attendant and shuffled awkwardly to our places in the darkened stands: a simple anonymous family, a family of spectators.

The show itself was enjoyable enough: a trained elephant, bowing on command; a dog parading around on two feet, dressed in a cape and wearing a cap with a feather and looking like an aristocrat; acrobats stretched out on gymnastics wheels like da Vinci's Vitruvian Man, careening around the ring in all manner of maneuvers; an Oleg Popov routine where he played a diminutive husband trying to make a little music with a trumpet while his much-larger wife bullied him with a massive slide trombone. Andrei snapped a few pictures trying to capture it.

"Don't waste film," I told him. "They're not going to come out well."

"He can take pictures if he wants to," Tamara said.

"It's dark, we're far away. He won't enjoy the pictures as much as he'll enjoy the show."

"He can take pictures if he wants to."

"Hush!" someone said behind us.

"We still need to take a family photo," I muttered.

Tamara gave a look but touched Andrei's shoulder. "Make sure you save some film."

"Can we go back to the monument after this?" he asked.

"Which one?"

"The one Papa took me to when we got the orange cosmonaut. The space monument."

"HUSH!"

"It's up to your father," Tamara whispered.

I checked my watch. We did, in fact, have time. We had all the time in the world.

Soon enough the show was over and we were back at VDNKh, jostling our way up the endless escalators, with me carrying Tatyana so we wouldn't lose her in the crowd. We exited into the bright warm summer afternoon. It was different than when Andrei and I had gone last; I was different.

On the pathway leading from the station to the monument they had finished construction of Cosmonaut's Alley. Imposing granite busts on massive pedestals. Gagarin and Tereshkova and Belayev. And, of course, Leonov. Andrei snapped pictures of all of them.

"Don't waste…" I started.

"Stop," Tamara said, low enough that I knew it was for me. "You wanted to go up there, you made it up there. Now you're jealous because you don't have a statue? How much is enough, Boris?"

I did not have an answer. But I tried. "Gagarin…"

"Gagarin's family has a statue and not a father. Would that make you happier? I know you're eager to get out of doing dishes, but…"

"Other families have both," I pointed out.

She did not like that.

"Let's get the picture here," Andrei said, with a nod towards the pedestal that said ALEXEI LEONOV.

"I don't know if this will be the best spot," I said. Nobody listened.

Andrei positioned himself to catch us next to the pedestal. "Hold Tatyana so she doesn't go anywhere."

"You want to be in the picture, yes?" Tamara said. "We'll get someone else to take it."

"Give the camera to a stranger?" Andrei eyed the ambling anonymous tourists, suspicious.

"Yes."

"What if they run off with it?"

"You're just like your father. No one is going to run off with it."

I'm sure I gave her a look. Finally I transferred my gaze to the stone Leonov. "It is quite a…flattering likeness. His hair's a good bit thinner these days."

"Well you've got him beat there, at least." She took the camera from around Andrei's neck and tapped an old woman on the shoulder to explain the situation, then darted back to join us in front of the pedestal. "Come on, Boris, that was funny. We need a smile for the picture."

I'm not sure I gave one.

The old woman was looking at the camera confusedly. "Do I have to press this?"

Andrei scampered over to show her. A momentary stay of execution—and my son was coaching the firing squad!

I shifted uneasily. "We're really going to do this?"

At last Tamara registered my intense displeasure. "Actually, let's take one over there instead." A nod towards the Monument to the Conquerors of Space.

Andrei dashed off toward it, his sister in tow. It was out of range of the old grandma so she handed the camera back and tottered away, relieved of duty.

"Thank you," I said to Tamara.

"I'm sorry. You were right, it was a bad spot." She gestured towards the obelisk. "I figured this one's your monument too, now."

I smiled. "It is, isn't it?"

"That would be enough for most men."

"I'm not most men."

We snagged down another bystander, a young man; we corralled the children together and stood there, the four of us, with the large titanium monument in the background, so much bigger than our family. The young man moved backward and crouched, struggling to fit it all in. I had never liked the photograph of Andrei and I under the East spacecraft, and I was skeptical as to how this one would turn out. Such a shame, how often one has to rely on strangers…

"Smile, everyone!" He shot a few frames and handed the camera back with a friendly nod.

"There's going to be a presentation this week," I told Tamara as we followed the children around the monument. "Brezhnev's giving us medals."

"There you go!" She smiled, seemingly happy at last.

"I know you're eager to go to the special stores…"

"I am happy for you, Boris." She took my hand; it did feel lovely. "I know how hard you've worked. I'm sure that will be nice, to finally be recognized."

My mood was improving; we got up to the monument and Andrei posed next to the statues in the frieze, striking optimistic socialist poses which his sister imitated in turn. I smiled, feeling again how my lips moved strangely over my false teeth. It was indeed my monument now; I had certainly earned it.

On the train home Andrei opened the back of the camera before he rewound the film. I saw the bare celluloid gleaming under the train lights, bombarded by photons, ruined.

"Andrei!" My voice spiked. The family photo, taken after all that effort, gone: perhaps it had been a good one after all.

He almost cried. "It was an accident!"

"It's all right." Tamara rubbed his shoulders. "It's only pictures."

For a couple minutes I stewed. Then I took a breath, patted him on the back. It was indeed only pictures. And I should not have been surprised: always in my story there were these moments, when triumph proved flawed or short-lived, when it was yanked from my grasp.

I consoled myself with the knowledge that there were more moments to come. A medal from Brezhnev: that would be nice.

•••

The night before the ceremony I stayed up late polishing my boots to a high gloss—arm wormed inside one boot, then the other, to hold the leather taut as I worked them over with the brush. Then: water in the lid of the tin of polish, and my oldest and softest undershirt, patterned now with fingerprints from past polishings. Over infinite repetitions the actions had become automatic: index and middle finger pressed together in a clean spot on the well-worn (and therefore gentle) shirt, with the rest of it twisted and wrapped around and clenched in the other fingers to keep the polishing surface smooth; shirt-covered fingers daubed first into the water and then the polish, pressed in such a way that it wasn't caked on but rather clung lightly to the dampened fibers; polish applied in circles, with the cloth-covered fingers working it into the leather such that it was cloudy at first but then smoothed to a nice clear shine.

I eyed the rest of my uniform carefully. Shirt ironed, with no hanging threads; medals perfectly aligned on the khaki tunic, and room at the top for one more, a golden star hanging from a red ribbon: Hero of the Soviet Union.

Then I placed everything carefully so I could be ready in the morning: tunic and shirt and trousers hung on the closet door, with the pants placed precisely on the hanger so as to maintain their crease; boots placed beneath them at first but then, after further reflection, set backwards in the back of the closet so Tatyana couldn't accidentally scuff them if she wandered in in the middle of the night. Finally it was my day to be recognized; I was leaving nothing—absolutely nothing!—to chance.

In the morning Brezhnev toured Star City; we—the four of us: Beregovoy, Shatalov, Yeliseyev, and myself—stood there waiting for the arrival, watching as the Zil limousines rolled up, flanked by a phalanx of motorcycle police, a flying formation of speed and power. We followed along as Brezhnev ambled down the concrete walks, chatting with the director as photographers hovered about, angling for this shot or that; we watched the silver-haired man with his distinguished tan face as he waved to the clots of people who had gathered outside the security cordon. Then: into buildings and through rooms, every familiar place made strange by the crush of bodies.

At last: the motorcade. Off to the Palace of Congresses for the presentation.

Down the highway we rolled, all of it cleared for our passage. Crowds lining the wide boulevards, massive apartment blocks hazy in the summer sun. The four of us in a black convertible, up front.

"You should stand now," the driver said, and we placed our hats at our feet so they wouldn't blow away, and we stood and waved to the people who were waving at us.

"It's not like it was for Gagarin," Yeliseyev said.

Beregovoy grunted. "Nothing ever will be."

"Maybe when we land on the moon," I chimed in.

"This is nice, though," Shatalov said. "No traffic."

"Traffic is for the little people," Yeliseyev said.

After all I'd been through, and all Beregovoy had done to botch the mission, it didn't seem fair that the four of us were each receiving the same medal, but I pushed those thoughts away and waved to the happy crowds. And I thought of the scene coming up in the Palace of Congresses: the golden brocade on the walls, and all the deputies and party functionaries applauding loudly, all of them there for us. At last, it was happening. It was happening, at last.

Onward we rolled, the motorcade unstoppable, all the motorcycle police with their shiny machines and white helmets gleaming in the sun—engines roaring, intimidating; belching acrid smoke that somehow only added to the excitement. Our car first, and Brezhnev behind us in a hard-top black limousine, and others further back: a carload of cosmonauts, Komarov and Tereshkova and Nikolayev and Leonov. All of them there for us.

And now, down the Kremlin Embankment, the river shimmering in the white summer sunlight and on the other side, those red brick walls with their imposing crenellations.

They meant something new now, for we had been chosen to be at the center of it all.

We made the turn, and so did the car behind us and a few motorcycles, but the rest of the motorcade headed onward. It seemed strange.

But then there it was, the Borovitsky Gate, and on the other side a crowd, the largest yet, cheering and clapping and waving Soviet flags; we drove through the dark tunnel and into the sunlit roar of the anonymous faces: all of them there for us!

The first gunshot sounded like a motorcycle backfiring.

But then came another and another and another, *BANG BANG BANG*, and I turned and there he was, a uniformed policeman, two pistols leveled, *BANG BANG*, firing straight into the Zil, *BANG BANG*, shattering glass and punching holes in the metal, *BANG BANG*, driver slumping, dead, Brezhnev maybe too, *BANG BANG*, that car veering wildly, crowd parting like the Red Sea, *BANG BANG*, motorcycle engine revving as the next guard in the phalanx sped up, the engine roar echoing off the buildings and punctuated by the soft sound of impact as he slammed into the assassin and sent his body flying like a rag doll and his pistols clattering to the paving stones, those noises immediately swallowed by the crowd's fevered screams.

By that time I was crouched low in the back seat, peering over the horizon of the limousine's trunk, with Beregovoy looking down at me with a smirk, saying: First time? And Yeliseyev saying: Fuck, did they just kill Brezhnev? And

Shatalov: No, he was further back, his car peeled off at the gate. That was Leonov and the others.

The next few hours blended into a blurred nothingness, all the myriad images flickering past so fast they became indistinct. How could they register, after what we'd just seen? But we did still have the ceremony. That was the strange thing: we did still have the ceremony.

It wasn't in the Palace of Congresses; it was a smaller wooden room. We found ourselves in there, and everyone was milling about, and when Leonov came in the room organized around him—there were pinprick wounds on his face from the broken glass, and a furrow of burned and torn cloth where a bullet had grazed his tunic.

Everyone wanted to talk to Leonov. I couldn't blame them at that point.

And the people continued to mill about and chatter, but it seemed the ones talking most were the ones who had seen the least. And we still had to wait for the man himself, but before he arrived my family was brought in, and we hugged wordlessly, and then trays of food appeared, and we ate mindlessly.

They had stopped the trains into the city, someone said. Word had gone out through official channels that someone had stolen a police uniform and two pistols, and the powers-that-be were worried that someone was plotting a terrorist attack. That's why Brezhnev's car and the others had turned away at the last minute; that's why they hadn't followed us through the gate. And that's when I realized how un-important we truly were.

At last he came in, the man himself. Around him, an entourage, a cloud of chatter and activity that preceded him into the room. He wore a gray suit and his hair was streaked with gray, and his face was tanned and lined.

He walked right past me, straight towards Leonov. I could not hear what he said but it sounded like an apology.

Eventually the room sorted itself out—someone must have been giving directions, but I really don't recall—and our families were watching and the flashbulbs were flashing and Brezhnev was going down the line pinning medals on chests, and when he got to me he tottered a little, and I caught a whiff of vodka on his breath. "Thank you for putting yourself in danger," he said.

And there it was on my chest: Hero of the Soviet Union. The second-most memorable thing to happen to me that day.

•••

They put me in the lunar program after that, at least. I had flown a rendezvous; that would be a valuable skill.

They did not give me a commander's slot. That was a crushing blow. Before I was a cosmonaut I had been making rough-field landings in the MiG-15, setting down on unpaved dirt strips; I was the best in the regiment. And what rougher field could there be than the moon?

And of course it was Leonov for the first mission. Of course. I was a backup again: my eternal curse.

But then, a month before launch: the accident.

Two helicopters, Mi-4s. Two crews, scrambled. Prime commander and backup flight engineer, backup commander and prime flight engineer. We would cut the power at 110 meters and the commander would autorotate down, quickly picking a landing spot. The whole point was that they did NOT want us working together, for that exercise at least; it would be a surprise for the commander when we cut the power. Temporary crews, built on distrust. Leonov and Volynov, Bykovsky and Makarov: names that did not look right next to one another. Not yet.

We practiced every month; at first I clenched my lips over my false front teeth as I watched the grass of the field rise up to meet us. Later I grew numb. Juddering hard landings. We practiced, and Leonov got very good. I had to admit, he got very good indeed.

And then last month, the accident. We saw it from above.

The way the tail boom bent. The way the fuselage spun sideways and angled itself up before crashing back to earth.

The bloom of flame against the green of the field.

We did not practice any more after that.

Alone on the Moon

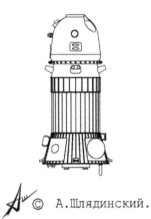

© А.Шлядинский.

"Eagle-2, Control. We've lost communications with the lunar lander. Over."

I hear the words as I come up on one more earthrise: the routine that is anything but. It was bound to go wrong sooner or later. With me involved, it was bound to go wrong. "Control, Eagle-2. How long has it been? Over."

An anxious breath. Then: "Eagle-2, just a few minutes. Over."

I return to the scene in my mind: Alexei climbing over the rim of the crater, exploring the moon beyond. Once the rim eclipsed the Lunar Craft, it would cut off the transmission path from his suit antenna. "He must have stepped out of line-of-sight."

The words travel their path. Then: "Eagle-2, not just him. The lander itself. We had some strange electrical readings. Trying to make sense of it. Over."

The electrical system. Redundant batteries, redundant controllers. Everything tested and retested. And yet… "Have you tried him on the suit freq…"

"Eagle-2, wait one. Over." Then: "There it is, back online!" Not quite cheers in the control room, but audible relief. "Eagle-1, Control. Radio check. Over."

I am still not listening on the relay. Too much chatter? Or do I just like imagining the responses? In the wait I see Blondie calling back to Earth and getting no response. Then walking back to the crater rim so he can see the Lunar Craft and calling again: still no response. And perhaps the edge gives way. Or he negotiates the treacherous rim successfully— how rarely do accidents happen when we're expecting them!—and then picks up too much speed bounding down the inside slope to get back to the silent lander. Unpredictable soil, a mis-planted footstep. A long slow tumble: gray moon and black sky in lazy succession. Does he feel fear, even for a moment? Surely. But he would never admit to it.

"Eagle-1, copy. Are you all right? Over."

I fill this gap with: what? Hope, or anxious prophecy. My rational mind reminds me: nothing bad ever happens to Blondie. But something must have happened.

Control again, anxious: "Eagle-1, is there damage to the suit? Over."

Did it really happen the way I predicted? A fall on the way back? It must have happened.

"Eagle-1, that is quite a relief. I'm glad they included that on the suit."

During Mishin's paranoid reign he'd imagined a cosmonaut falling flat on his back on the bulky life-support pack, and then being stuck on the moon like an overturned turtle. So they'd added a metal hoop to help the fallen cosmonaut roll over. Most of us had considered it unnecessary, a bit of mothering by engineers too anxious to ever fly themselves...

"Eagle-1, I'm sure that's true, but it's time to head back. Over."

Leonov trying to negotiate for more time? After electrical issues *and* a fall?

"Eagle-1, we do understand. Please commence close-out. Over."

More delay.

"Very well, Eagle-1."

I have to know. "Control, Eagle-2. How did we lose communications? Over."

A long lazy response. "Eagle-2, it was a mistake on our end. Over."

A complete brush-off. Absolutely insufficient. My blood pulses. "Control, Eagle-2. What kind of mistake? Over."

"Eagle-2, a fight controller sent a repoint command to the high-gain and typed in a wrong angle. We had to send a reset through the omnis. Over."

"What about the electrical issues? Over."

"We think it's a bad controller. We'll have him check when he gets back inside. Over."

This all sounds plausible. Unsatisfactory, but plausible. And there are redundant controllers. But still...

I breathe. Try to relax. I won't get anywhere butting heads with Control.

To keep myself busy I photograph Langrenus, coming up now. There is a poignancy, knowing I'll be leaving soon. How sharp will the memories be? A photo: Is it ever enough? Another exposure, another roll of film. I find myself curious if my memory is stronger than his. If mine is more accurate. My disappointments—I can tell that chain of stories any time of day. But in truth the imagery is no movie; unless I embellish, it feels flatter than magnetic tape, less real than celluloid. I have some dialogue committed to memory; I can see a few snippets of film: the East-5 launch, the solar panel antennas on Union-2, the assassination attempt. The accident. There must have been more. And sometimes when I revisit those places I can see other images: Andrei trying to lift the cannonball, or staring out the train window. But when I am, say, looking around at the train itself, I cannot believe things are as they were—the shape of the seats, the brightness of the lights. So I end up wondering: Did it change in my absence? Has it always been like this? And so, eating away at the edges of the memories, the acid thought: Did it really happen that way? And worse: Does it matter? If the memories keep shifting and I can't imprint them with sufficient force on my wife, my children, anyone? If they're transmitted haphazardly, if they fade without ever really leaving me...

I park the camera in the airspace over my head, make it wait like an aircraft in a full traffic pattern over a fouled runway.

Out the porthole I stare, my eyes as close to the glass as I can get them. Northwest of Langrenus, a triangle of craters. My triangle. Although they already look less dramatic than when we arrived: the sun is higher, the shadows, shorter. But I tell myself I will remember. I will remember thi...

"Eagle-2, Control. Radio check. Over."

"Control, Eagle-2. I'm still here. Over."

A wait while I wonder what they make of that fact.

"You've been staying off the relay."

"I need a little quiet. Over."

"Very well. So you know, we'll have him inside soon. He'll take his rest period and lift off next orbit, as planned. Over."

"Copy, Control." Proper, but hopefully curt enough to shut them up.

I know I'll have one last silent pass over the far side. Something to savor before rendezvous. And then: never again.

• • •

"...ladder is more slippery than it was on the way down. Over."

Leonov's end of the conversation picks up mid-sentence as I appear over the horizon. Does this mean it's over? While I wait for their response my mind cycles through the briefings, trying to remember the exact sequence of events: all those steps printed on his checklist and not mine.

"Eagle-1, Control. You should kick the dirt off your boots before getting back in the spaceship. Over."

"Who cares if I make a mess? No one will ever see it. Over."

This is the end. There is something sad in that. Still I want to get on with it. There is so much yet that might go wrong…

"Eagle-1, take care of your spacecraft. We're not discarding it yet."

Yet. Another reminder of everything we can't take home.

"Control, the camera is inside. I'm stepping back on the surface for just a moment. Attaching the hook to the sample box. Over."

"Eagle-1, Eagle-2," I interject. "Yes, please don't forget the camera! Over."

Imagine: what if he didn't take any photos? I smirk, picturing him at some party, years from now, balder still, chest covered in those absurd medals, drink sloshing as he gestures: *I was busy, I had other things on my mind. Perhaps I can interest you in a painting.* Whatever he does, he'll be explaining it for the rest of his life.

"Eagle-2, we'll have plenty of pictures." Then: "Knocking off dirt. It does get caked in the tread of the boot. Powdery, like graphite. But abrasive."

Control again, chatty. "You should bring some back for the rest of us!" No radio discipline. "That sandbox in the playground by the apartments. We could fill it up!"

And now I feel like everyone's taking it for granted that things are wrapping up successfully. Just like on Union-2—what a foolish feeling!

Still I do want to be a part of it.

"Control," Blondie says, and then a long crackle of static.

For his benefit I speak: "Eagle-1, say again, over."

"We might go over the mass budget! If I bring home that much dirt. Over."

"Yes, Eagle-1!" Again, Control. "They are partying in the streets, but we still have to get home! Over."

"Very well, Control. Let's finish this well. I'm at the top of the la..." More static.

Still the meaning is clear. He has taken his last steps on the moon. My future is now his past. Unless...

"Eagle-1, we are seeing strange electrical readings. Take a look when you get inside. Over."

"Control, the box is..."

He is gone in a crackle of static. I have to picture the rest: hauling himself inside, weighing his catch with a plain spring-loaded fishing scale, radioing Control so they can calculate placement...

Then again, there was something in his voice. Urgency.

From Earth: "Eagle-1, please repeat your last. Over."

I look down at the moon: still bright. Check the day sheet for the radio window, check the clock. It does seem strange that I've lost communications this early.

"Eagle-1, communications check. Over."

No response. I should hear it, his response. I should still have line-of-sight. What was it Control said about electrical issues?

"Control, let me try." Then before they can respond: "Eagle-1, come in, over."

Nothing. There is something disturbing about this.

The ragged line of shadow moves inexorably toward me. Earthglow still on the other side, cool and melancholy. But there is a darkness to the darkness.

• • •

For the next few minutes I switch to the relay channel and hear: call, and no response. Call, and no response. A cold fist grips my chest.

Then: "Eagle-2, this is Control. We've lost contact with the Lunar Craft."

More real this time. "Are you getting data at least?"

An anxious wait. Two seconds, but each one brings me closer to the far side, closer to being out of contact myself. Alone and unable to help.

"Eagle-2, we have no data. We have set the reset command through the omnis. We have sent it twice."

I am trying to picture the chain of failures that would have lead us to this point. Summoning documents about cycle-life testing in silver-zinc batteries. Causes of issues: weak welds on connections (tab-to-plate, tab-to-cell, tab-to-terminal); extraneous active material causing a short circuit between plates; rupture of the casing leading to loss of electrolyte. Maybe if his landing was a little too hard...

Still, there are three batteries, any one of which should be able to provide enough power. Redundant controllers. Everything has been tested and retested. And it *was* working.

"Control, were the battery temperatures nominal? Over." He landed in a crater. If the bottom of the lander was in shadow, if the heaters weren't working properly...

"Eagle-2, we are analyzing that data. Over."

Coming up below: the blackest darkness. The pseudo-terminator between the earthlit quadrant and the one with no earth and no sun. The milky vastness of the starlit universe.

I don't have time. He must still be down there. Unless there was something truly absurd—an explosion of the Block-E, maybe—he must still be down there.

"Control, have you tried him on the suit frequency? Over."

"We're trying now, Boris." A slip. But it feels appropriate.

Earth disappears before I know. I am alone in the darkness.

•••

In the silence I fly, impotent and brooding. Suspended in the firmament. Above, the whole universe. Below, the void. All of it unreachable.

I cannot be here. I cannot keep my mind in the here and now. I am trying to see the problem through prophecy, and solve it through pure waves of worry.

An explosion of the Block-E. That would surely destroy the Lunar Craft. Possibly kill him. If there were a weld somewhere that cracked on landing, and his reentry into the module disturbed it; if one of the tanks were leaking...a drip, so very slow in the low gravity; hypergolics igniting on contact, even on the airless moon. The lander consumed by cataclysm, this strange vacuum hellfire. And the ghost of Korolev hovering above, his big head repeating his mantra: *I warned you, did I not? I told you that stuff was the devil's venom.*

But could it really happen that way? To keep the center of gravity low on the Block-E, they did not stack the tanks as on a normal rocket but rather made the oxidizer torus-shaped, like a bagel, with the fuel like a ball hovering over the middle. Some vertical overlap, but if the fuel leaked it should drip from the round bottom and fall harmlessly through the torus's middle. And if the oxidizer leaked it would be too low and far outside to touch the fuel. Unless one or the other was spraying out, under pressure...

Sailing onward through the empty night ocean, through nothing. Towards: what?

The descent batteries. Could they all have failed at once? Extremely unlikely. Even if damaged on landing, surely one would fail first. So, too, the controllers. They thought one was having issues. If it failed, and the other was faulty? Maybe.

I think back to my chain of disappointments. Every link, every mission I've touched. East-5 and Sunrise-1 and Sunrise-3 and Union-2. What does it mean, to add this on the end?

Still it is unfinished. The metal circle not complete, the loop not pressed together. Not yet.

Pyrocartridges on Union-2. Failing to fire properly, failing to separate the modules. Pyrocartridges on the Lunar Craft, to separate the lander from its no-longer necessary legs, and everything else that would be staying on the surface. (High-gain antennas! Descent batteries!) Could those have fired too early?

It seems impossible. But it would explain everything.

Onward the orbit. A lonely fast sunrise. The bright unstoppable terminator, the harsh sunlight on the pockmarked surface. I thought it would be my last one alone, my last one to savor without Blondie jabbering on the radio, talking through the rendezvous. If he cannot lift off, I may get more time to myself. I cannot think of a more distasteful thought.

But the loop is not complete. Not yet.

• • •

Below, the bright craters scrape slowly by.

205

At last Earth peeks lazily over the horizon, as if reluctant to help. Still even it is powerless to go backwards.

"Control, Eagle-2. Have you heard anything? Over."

The words fly slowly. But they do find their mark. "Eagle-2, Control." I do not recognize the voice. "We need you to switch to the backup frequency. Over."

The backup frequency? Dear God. I grab my binder, slice my knifelike hand into the fanned weightless pages, riffle through them to find the right one, and dial in the changes as fast as my fingers can manage. Finally: "Control, Eagle-2 on backup. Any contact with Eagle-1? Over."

In the wait I run my fingers through my weightless hair. *You look like a circus clown*, Blondie had told me during the first orbit: the balding man mocking what he could not have. Still I cannot believe how anxious I am to talk to him again. I never would have believed it, but I'm eager.

At last: "Eagle-2, we are talking to him now. Over."

Relief. My hand starts kneading out the tension in the back of my neck. "Control, that is great news. Over."

"It's a start. We're still getting a handle on the situation. Over."

"Control, was it the pyrocartridges? Over." No comfort in this vision: I am now imagining the severed ascent stage tilting sideways in the base of the legs. Which way would it slip? What systems would be damaged? Could it fall all the way over?

After the wait: "Eagle-2, that is one possibility. He's back outside investigating. Communications are spotty talking through the suit antenna, so we're keeping that channel clear. Over."

"Copy, Control." Was I right? I must have been right. And did I know he hadn't taken his last steps on the moon? I must have known. Conflicting feelings, but any satisfaction feels slim, and easily crushed by the heaviness of everything else. So much worry. And so much worry to banish, by interrogation and action. "He'll need to get back inside if he's going to lift off this orbit. Over."

A long slow silence. Then: "Eagle-2, we are not planning on a liftoff this orbit. Over."

"Control, what do you mean? If the ascent batteries are good we can still rendezvous. Over."

I cock my head as if it will hasten their response. The words can't travel fast enough.

"Eagle-2, we've got Shatalov running through scenarios in the training mockup. We need a good plan before we send him back in. Over."

Typical of Control. Pretending they have it. Gaming out scenarios while events happen without them. "But the suit life…he's got to be low on O2. Over."

Are they annoyed I'm not playing along? I read many emotions into the communications delay. Finally: "Eagle-2, there are many factors to consider. We've got Shatalov running through scenarios in the training mockup. Over."

Onward I fly, Earth rising high in my black sky, then cut off by the window of my spacecraft. Their meaning, clear: *we'll call you when we need you. But we don't need you yet.*

Are they waiting for me to acknowledge their take on the facts? To acknowledge the facts themselves? Those are simple: I cannot talk to Blondie without their permission and assistance. Not yet, anyway. "Copy, Control."

This should be it from them. But no. "Who'd have thought, Boris?"

"Control. Unclear your meaning. Over."

"Who'd have thought you'd be the lucky one on this mission?"

I ignore this. Run my hand through my weightless hair: the action of a man who can take no action. They've got to launch him this orbit. They've got to.

•••

Below the movie repeats, not caring if I'm watching. I want to do something. I can do nothing.

The night before launch, Blondie had wanted to relax and screen a film. *White Sun of the Desert*, the new Eastern; he'd heard it was good, so he'd arranged for a showing in the projection room. But I had seen it with Tamara the week before, our last night together; besides I had too much to do. And in truth I did not want to spend *more* time with him. But now I can't help thinking of it. A new desert under the same white sun. Frivolous entertainment: how distant a concept. I'm unlucky in death, maybe I'll be lucky in love.

Below the movie repeats. Langrenus. My triangle, meaning unclear now. The near-side surface, the same size as the Soviet Union, but so little of it known. I do not care about getting back here; I do not care about anything but this. Still I can do nothing.

But I can do something soon.

I can switch to the suit frequency myself, talk to him once I'm above his horizon. A twelve-minute window. Control can't close it.

Back to the binder. To the suit frequency, now. The chain is not finished; the last loop is not closed.

Coming up on the time. The radio comes on: "Eagle-2, Control. We wanted to give you an update..." I turn the dial, cut them off. I only seek my own advice.

"Blondie, this is Boris. Come in. Over."

The voice: distant but real. "Boris! What a pleasure to hear from you!"

As if he wasn't where he was. As if this wasn't happening. Maybe I should try to be that way. "This is quite a way to get more time on the surface. Over."

"There is a lot to see! You should drop down for a visit."

His tone: too jovial? Hypoxia? I recall sessions in the high-altitude chamber, stern cosmonauts giggling like drunks. "You need to get inside. Lift off this orbit. Over."

"Boris, I'll get up there soon. Control wants me outside. It seems..."

Control now: "Eagle-2, what are you doing on this frequency? Over."

"Control, we need to get him inside. Pressurize the LVA and get him off the surface. Over."

I wait for them. I don't know why I wait for them.

Their response sounds like I do when Andrei won't listen. "Eagle-2, you need to switch to backup. Over."

"Control, he sounds hypo…"

"Eagle-2, clear this channel immediately! Over."

Reluctantly I comply. Turning the knob feels like closing the lid on a coffin. What are they going to tell me that they don't want him to hear? "Control, Eagle-2 on backup. He sounds hypoxic! Over." I wait for them to acknowledge this, at least.

Then: "Eagle-2, we can't talk while he's inside. The high-gains have no power, and the interior is cutting off the suit radio. Over."

As if I said nothing. My anger spikes. "Control, he sounds hypoxic! His O2 won't last another full orbit!"

A long pause. Longer than it should be. "Eagle-2, we are well aware of the O2 limits. We're running liftoff computations on the BESM-6. We need those to finish before he goes back inside. Over."

I shake my head. "Can he even write them down?" Surely they have to acknowledge this question!

But no: "Eagle-2, we also need to watch the ascent battery time. If we power up too soon and his spacecraft dies before it can reach you, we won't be any better off. Over."

For a moment I think of pressing on. Then as this sinks in: a reluctant breath. A nod they cannot see. We are being squeezed from all sides. "Control, I am well aware of the battery limits. Over."

I wait. What will be my punishment for ignoring the almighty?

At last: "Eagle-2, we know you want to talk to him. You can go ahead now. Over."

The dark edge of the Ocean of Storms looms below. Did we curse ourselves by landing here? I switch back to the main frequency.

"Blondie, I'm back now. Over."

"Boris! I hope they didn't curse you out on the other channel."

"Nothing worse than I get from Tamara." Again my absurd vision: the LVA toppling as he climbs aboard, the spacecraft tilting from its cradle and falling sideways to the surface. "Is the Lunar Craft stable?"

"It is in fair shape. I landed at an angle but the Block-E flange is still seated in the ring. We just need my liftoff time for the next orbit."

"I'm sure they'll tell you as soon as they have it, Blondie."

"I can see you! I can see you moving across the sky!"

"Let me try again to see you." Through the sextant attachment I look once more. The best I can hope for is a quick glint of metal, but I imagine I will somehow spot him personally, his spacesuited body jumping and waving like a child. "What are you doing...gymnastics while you wait?"

"No. I am resting. We need to conserve my oxygen." His voice suddenly sounds tired, more so than I realized. "I am resting and enjoying the view. Over."

Resting. Oh no. "How is the air in your suit? Over."

"It is a little thick."

"Do you have a headache?"

"I have had a little one for the last hour. It could be the brightness..."

The CO_2 scrubbers. I was worried about the O2, but if the CO_2 scrubbers are getting saturated... "Blondie, don't rest out there."

"Boris, I..."

He should know as well as I do what the dangers are. But if he's tired, if he isn't thinking straight, if his air is getting bad... "Whatever you do, don't rest." Is Control listening?

"Boris, it is..."

"If you need to get back inside and pressurize the LVA, don't wait for Control! They want to stretch out the batteries, but if you're getting tired, get inside!"

"Eagle-2, Control, we are monitoring this conversation, and..."

"Don't wait for Control, Blondie!" My words need to pierce the thick air, the deadened skull. "If you need to get inside, get inside! Don't w…"

"Eagle-2, Control, please switch to backup immediately!" I have never heard them this mad. But they are late; I am closer.

"Control, Eagle-1, I…"

"Eagle-1, we need to clear this channel! Eagle-2, it is vital to the success of this mission that you get back on the other frequency, immediately!"

"Blondie, don't wait!" A last plaintive plea.

Before they can respond I turn the radio all the way off. Breathe for a minute. The clock ticks, inexorable; I'm almost over his horizon anyway. I am wondering if I've spoken to him for the last time.

•••

"…gle-2, Control. Come in. Over." When at last I turn the radio back on, their tone is calmer than expected.

I wait. Why do I wait?

Again: "Eagle-2, Control. Come in. Over."

"Control, Eagle-2." Feigned calm. "How may I help you?" And feigned pleasantries. What will they make of it?

"Eagle-2, that was not acceptable. You need to let us solve the problem. There are a lot more brains in this room than on your spacecraft. Over."

Breathe.

"Copy, Control."

Breathe and wait.

"Eagle-2…" An exaggeration of the number. "Nobody flies alone. Nobody gets up there on their own. And if you ever want to get up there again…"

"I don't care, Control." I interrupt them even though I cannot interrupt them; their words have flown. "I want this to end well. Nothing matters after that. Over."

A pause while the words find their mark. "Kamanin might hold you to that. Over."

"I don't care, Control. I want this to end well." I gaze at the dim bluish surface, the night moon scene. Not mine.

"Eagle-2, we all want the same thing. You have to trust that. Over."

A deep breath. A silent weightless nod.

•••

We still have a fair amount of time until blackout, but Control and I seem quite content to ignore one another. It is evening in Moscow; I realize at last how long it's been since I've eaten, and how full my bladder's gotten. I am still a man, after all.

No snide comments or lewd jokes as I turn on the vacuum, insert my penis into the apparatus. There is a very substantial chance I will fly home alone. It is quite an unsatisfactory situation.

The American astronaut John Young did not discuss his feelings after Apollo 10, beyond the expected anodyne statement; the more they tried to interview him, the less he said. So there is a template for what I may end up facing. But I cannot accept that this will end the same way.

Relieved and with a clearer head, I wait for Control to need me. I wait and wait; surely they will need me before I need them. Signal loss soon; I will prepare my meal after that. I can wait that long.

What is happening on the relay channel?

I cannot abide not knowing.

I know I should stay, wait to be needed; I know I should be where they're expecting me. They have a lot to manage, and I should not add to it. But I also know they're not going to tell me if I'm right. My enemies will not give me that satisfaction.

I switch back to the relay frequency.

"...advised to ascend the ladder and pressurize the LVA. Liftoff at Moscow Time two-zero-four-nine. Please acknowledge. Over."

No response. Can he respond? I cannot abide not knowing. Even the thought of knowing in the future—that is not enough. I need to know now.

"Eagle-1, Control. Repeat transmission. You are advised to ascend the ladder and pressurize the LVA. Liftoff at Moscow Time two-zero-four-nine. Please acknowledge. Over."

My heart tightens. They were not going to tell me this. How long have they been calling? I should ask them, on the other channel. But will they tell me? Will I know? If they repeat it again I will know, more than whatever they will tell me on the other channel. If they repeat it again I will know.

"Eagle-1, Control. Repeat transmission. You are advised to ascend the ladder…"

I can't take it anymore. I switch back to backup. "Control, Eagle-2. Come in. Over."

Nothing. Where are they?

"Control, Eagle-2. Radio check. Over."

"Eagle-2, Control. We were wondering about you. We are coming up on signal loss. Over."

Earth is indeed dipping low in the black sky. "Control, Eagle-2. What is happening on the other channel? Over." It is my turn to bark at them. An insufficient satisfaction indeed.

They delay like a recalcitrant child. "Eagle-2, we received several garbled transmissions, right around the time we transmitted the computation results. We are trying to get a status. Over."

A status. So much meaning in that word.

"Control, this was…" I rub my eyes. So great the anger. So brittle the pride. "Control, what was his last transmission? Over."

I wait. Will they tell me?

"Eagle-2, wait one. Over."

They will not tell me. Still I wait. Count. One. Two. Three. Four. Five. "Control, Eagle-2. Just tell me what he said!"

Again the wait. "Eagle-2, Control. We are coming up on signal loss. Over."

I hear myself yelling. Against my will it is all flooding out. "Control, if you think you can keep me in the dark about this, you are sorely mistaken! I am going to find out when I get back! And I am going to talk, and the State Commission will listen! And when they find out…"

Here I finally notice: Earth has set. My words are going nowhere.

It is quite an unsatisfactory situation.

•••

Alone in the dark. Forty-eight minutes of silence. To think I wanted this. To think I wanted to savor it.

Is there still a chance this will all turn out right? If so, I need to eat now. But if so, it is just a chance.

I force myself to prepare a single dinner. Force the tasteless food into my mouth, force myself to swallow. The rippling of the involuntary muscles of the esophagus: that at least is taken care of.

As soon as I've choked down a few bites I start studying the rendezvous book. Case after case after case. I do need to be prepared. There is a chance I need to be prepared.

The darkness makes it hard to be hopeful. And it seems too obvious a metaphor for what is happening. But the laws of orbital mechanics and planetary motion do not care for what is trite or formulaic or over-the-top. They serve the same symbolism with methodical regularity, oblivious to their audience.

At last sunlight explodes through the window. The only options, it seems: not enough, or too much.

I turn my back to the scene, ignore the sharp pockmarked majesty below. I study the rendezvous book. Over and over and over.

●●●

Earthrise: how I long to be back! But not as a scapegoat, forever talked about in whispers from the other side of the room. Success: is it still possible?

"Control, Eagle-2, calling on backup. Do you have a status? Over." No need for preliminaries, no need for explanations. This is all there is.

I wait. No answer.

"Control, Eagle-2. I need a status. Over."

My whole life is stopped until I hear their transmission.

"Eagle-2, Control. We think he is back inside. Over."

A breath. Some relief. But: we think? "Control, Eagle-2. Unclear your meaning. Over."

At last: "We have him on the omnis. Communications are spotty but he seems to have powered up the LVA. Over."

I would celebrate, but for their tone. "Control, what is the problem? Over."

After the gap: "Eagle-2, power-up was earlier than we would have liked."

Of all the fucking things! "Control, I'm…" I clench my bare hand around the burning fuse just before the explosion. "I'm sure he needed to do it! Over."

I await their answer.

"Eagle-2, the ascent battery charge is not as expected. We are turning off systems. Trying to decrease the load. Over."

A deep breath. A head shake. Rubbing of the eyes. "Control, there is not much to turn off. Over."

"Correct, Eagle-2. We need to leave the rendezvous radar off for the ascent. He has life support, navigation, radio, and that's it. And he needs to lift off this orbit. Otherwise we have a dead lander."

"Copy, Control." I ball my fist. Unclench it. Spin my weightless body to look out once more at the hostile surface of the moon.

"Eagle-2, he is aligning the platform now. Lander position is as follows. Latitude: minus zero-point-zero-four-seven. Longitude: minus two-nine-point-one-three. Unfortunately the surface indicator is reading OFF. Over."

Great. The lander thinks it's already flying. "Control, I take it that's a problem. Over."

"Eagle-2, he'll need to…" (A wayward static crackle.)

"Control, please repeat your last. Over."

The wait. "Eagle-2, we need…" (Again the important part is garbled. It would be comical if we weren't in the thick of it.)

A frustrated head shake. "Control, I do not copy. Over."

Again the long pause. "Eagle-2, the engine restart program will not work. He needs to re…" (Again the static. Although now I think I understand.)

"Control, repeat your last. Over."

"He needs to reopen the shutoff manually! We also need a clean readback on liftoff time and plane change parameters once you're o…" (Again, radio noise. But I can guess the missing text: *over the horizon*.) "…by to copy. Over."

I open the binder. Prepare to copy. I do need to cooperate: so many things aren't. "Standing by. Over."

I wait, grease pencil in hand.

"Eagle-2, we have not gotten a clean readback. His numbers could be all wrong. You will have six minutes to get confirmation once you're over his horizon. You need to get confirmation! Over."

I explode: "Yes, Control! I understand! Let's get on with it!"

Pencil poised, I wait. What will they make of my impertinence?

"Eagle-2, liftoff time as follows…"

I copy methodically. There is a chance, and I have to remind myself it is bigger than it had been on the other side of the moon. But it is still just a chance.

●●●

I'm dimly aware of the movie replaying yet again outside the portholes. Empty Fertility. Tranquility: name like a cemetery. No time to watch and ponder. All I care about are the grease-pencil markings in my binder.

I flip over to the main channel and start transmitting a few seconds before the expected time. "Eagle-1, this is Eagle-2. Come in. Over."

No response. What did I expect?

Again: "Eagle-1, Eagle-2. Come in. Over."

Clenching of fingers. Muscles contorting, tips digging into my palm.

Finally: "Be patient, Eagle-2! I am very busy down here. Over."

The ass! I could choke him. "Eagle-1, we have a lot to talk through! You need to manually open the main shutoff to fire your engine. Over."

The clock is unstoppable. Relentless.

"Eagle-2, yes, they told me. Over."

His lazy tone throws me off. "They told you?"

"Yes, on the main channel, right before you came on. We finally got a clean transmission on the omnis."

Still the clock climbs. "Eagle-1, I also need a readback on liftoff time. Over."

"Eagle-2, I have the time! It is two-zero-four-nine plus one-five. Over."

"And the plane change."

Eagle-2, plane change is one-one meters per second, plus-y axis. Over."

I gaze down at my carefully copied markings. He was fine without them! Even the radio seems determined to put me in my place, by finally being reliable for Control.

Now the clock seems slow. We still have four minutes until the moment of truth. Four long minutes. Nothing matters until then. Reluctantly I transmit. "Eagle-1. How is it down there? Over."

"Boris." A long pause while he savors his power. "I told you I wouldn't tell you. I can't go back on that now!"

The ass. I can practically see the smirk. "Careful. You still need me to pick you up. Over."

"If I can get up. I pressurized the thruster system and we're very low. Over."

My sympathy comes flooding back. Of all the things! When will it stop? "Copy, low pressure on the thrusters. Over."

"You may have to do most of the flying, Boris."

"I'm up for it."

"I am ready to get off the surface, I can tell you that much."

"All right, let's do it." Below the surface sweeps by, an endless wave. This has to happen now, this orbit.

"Fuel Feed One: OPEN. Oxidizer Feed One: OPEN. Fuel Two: OPEN. Oxidizer Two: OPEN."

On the sharp airless surface I can see we are coming up on the Ocean of Storms, crossing rays of Copernicus. If this doesn't happen now, it's not going to happen.

Control calls, garbled: "Eagle-1, copy all…" The transmission dissolves.

"One minute readiness. Ready to open the main shutoff. Over."

Two seconds. "Copy, one minute readiness."

Still the relentless gray sweep. My heart pounds. This has to happen.

"Thirty seconds."

"Copy thirty." Again my hand is clenched; I look at it as if it belongs to a stranger.

"Ten seconds." Eternity. "Five seconds. Moving the valve. It's a little stuck…trying to get leverage…"

My heart spikes. "Blondie, you've got to fire!"

"Moving it…ignition!"

I close my eyes to see it, the delicate metal pod exploding into the black sky. I force myself to breathe.

"Trying to get centered…thrusters are firing a lot…"

Oh no.

"Mass placement...still off...thrusters are kicking...gauges are low..."

And I can see it, I can see him, the light golden spacesuit, body slumped, trying to stand and brace itself, swaying as the thrusters fire and the spacecraft claws its way into the black sky.

"And now we're pitching over...and we're picking up speed! That was fantastic! What a ride!" Whatever worry I heard in his voice is gone. "I could see my shadow on the moon! It looked like a bat, it looked fantastic! Like a black bat, sweeping across the gray surface! What a magnificent sight!"

He sounds like a kid at an amusement park. And just like that I am jealous again.

But only for a moment.

• • •

Soon the emotion fades from his tone. We are not yet free from worry. We are nowhere near free.

As he ascends he starts calling out landmarks. Craters and rilles. Speed and altitude. I follow along, ticking off numbers. Everything is yet to be determined.

"Heading down the mainline." Our nickname for one long east-west rille. "1000 meters per second."

"Copy, 1000."

The long wait. Every scenario in the rendezvous book has him in the high 1600s for a safe orbit. And in the same plane. We need to get there.

"Plane change complete."

"Copy, plane change." A small relief.

"1200."

"Copy, 1200." He needs to be in the high 1600s. But we know he ate into the reserve, landing.

"What do you think, Boris? Are we going to make it?"

The burden of prophecy. Will saying make it so, or jinx us? "I think we're going to make it."

"I think so too. 1400."

"How does it feel?"

"Boris…"

"This is ascent, you can talk about that."

"Like an elevator. 1500."

"Copy, 1500. Let's get there."

"And we are…engine cutting off. Not quite there."

I shake my head. "Eagle-1, give me a number, for God's sake."

"1590."

"Fuck your mother." Below the ragged terminator looms, spilling into the bottoms of ancient craters, ready to eat our day. Another bit of obvious symbolism, delivered without care. What does Control make of this? I'm surprised we haven't heard from them yet. "Control, we have Eagle-1 at one-five-nine-zero meters per second. Over."

They take their time responding. "Eagle-2, Control. We copy one-five-nine-zero. We're waiting on the BESM-6, but we believe that's a negative solution. Over."

Awful news, calmly delivered. A negative solution: he'll crash into the near side once we come around. "Eagle-1, do you copy?"

"Copy, Eagle-2." Surprisingly dispassionate. "I can probably get some more from the thrusters. Over."

"Eagle-1, we'll need those for maneuvering."

A bemused tone in his voice. "Not if we don't use them."

"How much do you have? Over."

"Very low. But I don't see any other options."

"Shouldn't we check with Control?" Out of sunlight completely now.

A pause. I imagine their response: *Oh, now Boris wants to listen to us.* And then: "All units, negative solution confirmed. Use whatever thrusters you need. Over."

"Very well. Commencing burn in the plus-x axis." Smooth and calm, like it's just an elaborate simulation. "1600...1620...numbers coming up...and thrusters are exhausted. Over."

"We need a number, Eagle-1."

"1645. Over."

That sounds good enough. Is it? "Control, did you copy? We are at one-six-four-five. Over."

"Copy, one-six-four-five. Over." An echo rather than an answer.

"Will that be enough?" As if they don't know what we're asking.

"Eagle-2, we are plugging the new numbers into the BESM-6. Over."

"Copy, Control."

A long wait in the pale darkness. Then: "Eagle-1, your orbit is one-zero-point-two kilometers by one..." (Garbled.) "...nt-four. Over."

He asks for both of us. "Control, Eagle-1. I did not hear the full second number. Over."

I am hoping against hope that there were two digits under the static. There have to be two, right?

But no. "One-zero-point-two by one-zero-point-four. Over."

Ten kilometers by ten. In my rendezvous book there are scenarios where I drop into a lower orbit to rescue him. But we've never calculated one that low. "Control, Eagle-2. Will that allow for a Case Nine rendezvous? Over."

Again the pause. "Eagle-2, the BESM-6 should have an answer soon. But there is one factor we can't plug in to the equations. Over."

"Control, what is that?" I ask although I know.

"Exactly how high the mountains are on the far side of the moon."

I know it but it hurts to hear it; we have more to think about than I thought.

I can look at the moon a little now, at least; I am a spectator again, for the moment. Below I see the far edge of the Ocean of Storms, bathed in Earth's pale glow; it is large and empty and calm. I am a spectator, but not disinterested: it may kill us yet.

The computer is calculating, 384,000 kilometers away. We should have all the answers soon. All the answers but one.

• • •

We fly around the moon, through the bluish earthlit quadrant. Mid-evening, by our biological clocks. We wait for a verdict.

It does occur to me that Blondie will be in the low orbit for a full revolution before I get down there. There is an unpleasant relief in the realization. If there are any terrain issues...

It is a dark thought. Needless to say I do not share it.

At last: "Eagle-2, Control. We have parameters for a Case Nine descent burn. We will send it to your spacecraft and have you copy. Over."

Again the rendezvous book. A page I had hoped not to use. "Standing by to copy. Over."

Always the silence. Now more than ever it sounds like hesitation. Maybe it is. "Eagle-2, please switch to backup for the parameters. Over."

I dial in the now-familiar frequency. "Control, Eagle-2 on backup. Over."

"Eagle-2, just so you are aware. You don't have to do this. Over."

I cannot hide my exasperation. "What else am I supposed to do? You think I can come back, knowing I didn't do my part?"

They don't know if I'm done. At last they respond. "Eagle-2, we need to tell you all the information. We…"

I step on their transmission. "Control…I won't be down at his altitude until we're back on the near side. Correct?"

The delay. "That is correct, Eagle-2."

"Well I hate to say it but…if there are terrain issues, he will find out soon. Over."

The wait. "Eagle-2…" Their hesitancy tells me much. "Eagle-2, based on the late ignition and thruster burns…we have to drop you into a lower orbit to catch up with him. Yours will be nine-point-five kilometers by ten-point-four. And the margin for error…" (Either the transmission is garbled, or it ends.)

Nine-point-five. Dear God. "Control, are those definite numbers? Surely you can keep me above ten. Over."

"Eagle-2, not with his battery and oxygen levels. If we go with a safer orbit his ship will be dead by the time you get there. Over."

"Copy, Control." I think of Tamara, Andrei, and Tatyana.

"Again, Eagle-2, you do not have to do this. You'll be alone on the far side, out of radio contact. If the time is coming, and you want to abort the firing...for safety reasons..."

I think of my wife; I know what she would say. Then I think of Blondie.

In any event, I only seek my own advice. "Control, just send the parameters. Over."

With the grease pencil I copy. Soon my fate is written. It just looks like numbers.

•••

Again the earth drops out of view; we are swallowed by the empty moon and the cold universe. Ordinarily I would see Blondie somewhere down there, a red light winking at me across the void. But we have left his rendezvous beacon off, to save batteries. Still he is down there. I think.

Half an hour ago, I was worried about coming home alone. Now I am worried about coming home, period. If I drop down to meet him and I am too low, will I ever know? Will I see the terrain for a moment, black against the stars, rising above the horizon? Will I see it then and know?

Maybe. Or maybe here in the dark quadrant it will be over in an instant. An invisible mountain, an end too fast to comprehend.

I won't be in the low orbit completely until after the circularization burn, back on the near side. And I do have the option, not to do it. I do have the option, not to take the chance.

But the announcement has been made. The country is already celebrating—possibly the planet. If I don't do it, I will be a scapegoat for sure.

Blondie is down below. A hundred and forty kilometers away, at least. Or he is gone, flown into the moon already: no explosion because there are no propellants left. A smear on some dark mountain.

"Eagle-2, this is Eagle-1. Come in. Over." A voice in the night. Still there. For now.

"-1, this is -2. Looks like it's just the two of us. Over."

"Sorry to interrupt your quiet time, Boris."

"What are you talking about? It's always a joy to hear your voice."

"You're a bad liar, Boris!"

At this I say nothing. It is good that he is still here, right? Although it means I have to make a decision which otherwise would have been made for me. And my orbit will be lower than his...

I will not know for sure, this orbit. I will not know anything for sure.

"You're awfully quiet up there. Over."

"It is a lot to think about, Blondie."

What do I expect from him? Anger? Pressure? Instead he just says: "It is a lot to think about."

Again I study the numbers. I can read them but I don't know what they mean. The darkest thought creeps: maybe Control knows the mission is lost; maybe they want me as a scapegoat. If I abort the burn I will be a live one, and that will be inconvenient for all concerned. But if they fly me into the moon, they can say whatever they want...and they could be flying me into the moon with this burn.

I watch the timer count down. Everything is ready. I watch it count down; I do not know to what.

I have the means to stop it. All I have to do is stop it.

I watch the timer count down.

●●●

When the S5.35 fires I feel it pushing into my back, heavier than I remembered. Union-2, on the pad: the rumble that told me it was finally happening. And now this is more real than that.

The numbers count down. The engine appears to be firing perfectly. But what is perfect, and for whom?

I monitor the burn. At the appointed time I bring my hand up to the panel; it hovers over the shutoff. If the burn is doing what they say, I still need to be able to cut it off if it goes on too long. We're dropping the low point on the near side, but if we lower it too much...

The S5.35 cuts off, exactly on schedule. Perfect. Assuming perfect means what they say it means.

I flow into sunlight, the bright quiet part of the orbit. I rotate the spacecraft just a little, to get a full view in the porthole. Already the craters look larger than they were.

A radio crackle. "Are you coming down here, Boris?"

I chuckle. I am so used to being on my own that I have not read anything off; I haven't transmitted a single word to let him know I have, in fact, completed the first part of the maneuver that might save his life. "I am coming down there, Blondie."

"Good. That is good to hear. You'll get to see the moon up close! It is an exciting place, I can tell you that."

As if trying to convince me to make a decision I've already made. "Did you think I wouldn't do it, Blondie?"

"You never know until it's done."

And down below I can see him at last, far ahead of me still, moving fast against the rugged craters. A dot, a glint of metal, a silver seed ejected from the sterile soil.

•••

The craters grow large and unfamiliar; they whip by faster and faster. It feels all wrong, to be getting closer to the moon this late in the mission. Again I have to wonder about Control.

At the lower altitude it takes longer to come out of blackout. But at last we hear them.

"Eagle-2, Control. It looks like a successful burn." They sound relieved.

"Looks can be deceiving."

They don't quite know what to make of that. I listen as they run the numbers through the BESM-6 to determine the parameters for the circularization burn; I copy diligently with the grease pencil. Conditioned like Pavlov's dog, responding immediately to the stimulus.

Below now, a new movie, dramatic: the pacing, much tighter; the plot, more compelling. I am busy but I cannot help glancing out the portholes here and there, trying to confirm what I think I'm seeing. My trio of craters looks bloated—distorted and strange, menacing even. I cannot even see Langrenus; the horizon is that much closer now.

For my own peace of mind I look through the sextant and check the alignment; I check and recheck and recheck. This second firing is even more dangerous; I'll be settling in at the lower altitude.

Eventually there is nothing more to verify. I strap back in and watch the timer count down to the fateful moment. Redemption or execution, I'm not sure which. But I can't avoid it now. Not with everyone watching.

When the S5.35 fires, it feels like a knife in the back. The old lie: just relax, and it will all be taken care of. At the burn's conclusion I mash the cutoff button, just to be sure; I am not trusting the timer any more than I have to.

"S5.35 firing is complete," Control says. "Orbital parameters are exactly as expected. You should be catching up with him soon. And we'll program one last burn. Over."

"Yes, I have him on radar now. Range is twenty kilometers. Over." Outside the portholes, the menacing scene. Even at my normal high altitude it had looked close and clear. Now it's near enough to touch. I almost feel a part of it now. I think of Apollo 10 and shudder: God willing, I won't be.

"Thank you, Boris," Blondie says.

"Don't mention it."

• • •

And now we're flying back into near-darkness, with him far ahead, still unseen. A night flight, fast and low, trusting the instruments even though every urge says no.

Through the earthlit quadrant we chat with Control intermittently as the distance slowly drops. They transmit the programming for the last piece of the rendezvous: a short burn on the far side to nudge me into the same orbit as my target. Then at the appointed time, the radio vanishes in a crinkle of static. If it all goes wrong, it will be some time before anyone even knows.

Eagle-1 comes on. "Well, Boris, once more it's just you and me."

"And nothing to see."

"When the window is pointed skyward I can see a lot, actually."

It takes a second for the meaning of this to hit. "Wait, you're tumbling?" Of course he hadn't mentioned this. Of *course*.

"It's a small rotation. Maybe a degree a second."

"With no thruster propellant to stop it."

"Well nobody's come by to top up the system."

Exasperation. "Are we going to be able to dock, even?"

"It's a small rotation. One axis."

In my mind's eye I inspect the docking apparatus, the pin and the plate. Somewhat forgiving of error compared to what the Americans had on Apollo. Still, not designed for rotation. And if he says a degree a second, it could be more like two or three. Or ten. If only I had thought to ask about this before the burn... "We're going to have a time of it. We won't be able to use the sensors to align even."

"You can still use the periscope and the screen. Do it visually."

"And if it fails?"

"I can float across the gap if I have to. If you get close enough."

"And if you miss?" I can picture it now, him floating free, me burning propellant chasing him across the sky. Because if I don't try, what will they say?

"I can do it with the tethers. Clip in on this end with one. Have the second one hooked to me, with one end in my hand. Float across and hook in, then release the first tether from my end."

"The tethers aren't that long. We're going to have a time of it." Outside the portholes, the nightscape does not look much different than it had on my last orbit. But it feels different. The void is no longer impassive: now it's angry. Or hungry, eager to swallow me. I watch the numbers on the radar altimeter undulate unpredictably. Here and there come spikes that take my breath away. How fast will it happen? I strain to look at the horizon, to see if I can spot bits of starscape being eclipsed by the black ragged mountains.

It occurs to me I could nudge the thrusters, just a little. Some forward momentum, enough to raise my orbit the tiniest bit. It would throw off the rendezvous solution but it might just save my life. And no one would ever know...

His voice snaps me out of my reverie. "What is my range?"

"Three kilometers now."

But he would know, wouldn't he? And I would know. For the rest of my life I would know.

"Copy, three kilometers."

I strain at the porthole. Is my angle right to catch him against the backdrop of stars? We should be closing in on the same altitude, so: maybe not. "I can't see you. Can we turn on your beacon now?"

"Copy, Eagle-2. Turning on the beacon."

And there he is ahead of me, a red light flashing, a vision of a glorious future perched uneasily on the knife edge of the ragged black horizon.

And then it goes out.

Panic.

Did he hit something?

"Eagle-1, this is Eagle-2. Radio check. Over."

No answer.

"-1, this is -2. Radio check. Over."

Nothing.

Panic.

Breathe.

Think.

He couldn't have hit something. I would have hit it too. At this speed, at this range, I would have flown into it before I had time to key the microphone.

But if our paths are still slightly divergent, if he's just a few hundred meters out of plane...

He couldn't have hit something. Right?

"Blondie, this is Boris. Come in. Over."

No response.

A sudden bump—jarring. My body falling backwards, hitting the bulkhead. Did I actually collide with something? Then I remember: the last little burn they'd programmed, to finish the rendezvous.

If there's anyone to rendezvous with.

Coming up on midnight. I call in the darkness and get no answer. I call and call and call. I fly through the darkness alone.

•••

A few minutes later, sunlight hits, overwhelming: another improbable dawn. And yet there is something odd: in the orbital module, a strange shadow passes over the porthole.

I float over to investigate, and when I look out there it is, the dead spacecraft, perhaps fifty meters off and straight ahead in the sun.

Still nothing on the radio. I strap in, pulse the thrusters, maneuver closer to get a better viewing angle. It is tumbling very slowly, just like he said; it looks strange now, no legs, a short metal bone: thin in the middle and larger at both ends.

I pull out the camera. I want proof that it happened, proof I did my part. I am raising it to my eye when:

Movement.

A gloved hand waving in the window, glimpsed in an instant.

"Blondie!" I call out. I don't care if he can't hear me. He's alive! "Blondie!" I call, and I am sure he shares my joy.

The window pitches back up into view and he is smiling and signaling. Helmet visor up, touching his ear, slicing his hand sideways and shaking his head. No radio?

I offer an exaggerated shrug like: What do you want to do? But his window is pitching up further and now he is out of sight.

When it comes back around he is no longer smiling. He makes the no radio sign again, then brings his gloved hands together, index fingers extended and touching tips.

Rendezvous! Of course, what else could he want to do?

"All right! Yes! Rendezvous!" I place my bare fingertips together like his and then nod.

And now I am tightening my seat straps, wearing the spacecraft like a tailor-fit suit. And I am translating again with the thrusters; he is gone from the porthole but now I have him on the periscope view screen; I am trying to judge the path his docking plate will take, the arc of motion that will allow my probe to penetrate it and capture.

I edge closer, as close as I dare: unplanned contact could cause problems for both of us. I see the docking plate, look at the distance. He is rotating faster than he said he was. I count backwards to calculate when I will need to start thrusting, what features from his spacecraft I will see on the viewing screen.

And: now. Now is the time.

A quick flick of my left hand and then: a shudder of metal transmitted through my seat. No indicator light.

Fuck.

On the screen I can see him tumbling, slightly faster now. And...did I push him away?

Fuck.

A gleam of the docking plate on the viewing screen. It's a fat target, almost the width of his spacecraft, like a flat hat. Perhaps the angle was too great at the last moment, perhaps the probe could not go straight through the slot...

No matter. We will get there.

I translate back around; now there is both pitch and yaw in his tumble, and everything feels off. Again I try to gauge the rotation; again I see my moment, or maybe it is not my moment; again I pulse forward and:

Another shudder, deeper now. And of course: no light.

Fuck. Fuck! Fuck fuck fuck fuck fuck.

I pull off and of course he is tumbling, three axes now, tumbling and moving away. A cruel problem in Newtonian physics, actions and reactions, transfer of momentum from a large massive spaceship to a much smaller and lighter one.

I have to make this happen. I have to make this right. It all depends on me.

I move in closer; I see the sunlit edges of his spacecraft flashing across the viewing screen. Can I judge when the plate will be in front of me? I have to try; I have to do this. I am back in position, ready to risk it all on one last desperate toss of the dice when:

On the viewscreen, a quick glimpse of a gloved hand, pounding flat on the window of the tumbling spacecraft. Meaning clear: STOP.

A quick rotation: now I can see the Lunar Craft out the porthole. But when the window tumbles past I do not see any signals; I cannot tell what he's doing in there. I unstrap and wait for earthrise.

•••

Fatigue floods in as I wait. It has been a long workday, far longer than expected; we should have been headed home already. I wait and wait. Surely only a minute or two, but it feels like much more.

Earth rises in the window.

"...ll units, Control. All units, Control. Please give us a status. Over."

"Control, Eagle-2. There appears to be an electrical failure on Eagle-1. We rendezvoused on the far side but he is tumbling and we have not been able to dock. I am keeping station with the thrusters. Over." I catch myself wondering: Could he be incapacitated? I glance out the porthole for an answer, but his window is turned away.

"Copy, Eagle-2. We are plugging orbital parameters into the BESM-6 and...it appears your orbit is unstable. Over."

"Control, how is that possible? Over."

A long wait, for a response I know I won't want. "Eagle-2, it could be mass concentrations or maneuver effects. But you will be almost a half kilometer lower by the time you get around to the far side. Given the altitude uncertainty...we're not sure it will be enough for a full orbit. We are going to send up commands for a near-side burn. Over."

A burn. If I separate from the Lunar Craft... "Control, he's not...I can't just leave him here."

Two seconds. Then: "Eagle-2, do you have any other options?"

"Control, I…" I look to the porthole. On the Lunar Craft, the hatch is edging open, a black crescent moon, like it was in my mind when he landed. It rotates out of view. "Control, we are going to attempt an untethered spacewalk."

"Eagle-2, do you have a time estimate? We need to realign soon. Over."

"No, we haven't had communications, we…" The hatch turns back into view; now I see a helmeted head, and a hand pointed insistently at the side of it. Adrenalin sparks my fogged mind: the suit frequency! Oh, for fuck's sake. "Control, wait one."

And I turn the knob and there he is. "…gle-2, this is Eagle-1, calling on suit radio. Repeat. Eagle-2, this is Eag…"

"Eagle-1, Eagle-2, I hear you loud and clear! Over."

"Eagle-2, I was wondering when you'd figure it out!"

"Eagle-1, you could have talked us through the rendezvous."

"I needed to conserve suit power. It is well past the margins. I couldn't maneuver an…"

"Eagle-1." I step on his transmission. "They are planning a burn. We might crash into the far side if they don't do it. And they need to realign first."

"Well let's not waste time talking. I am clipping the tether to the lander."

His plan: tethers still. Possible before, with the slower tumble, but now... "I don't know if that's..."

He steps on me this time. "I'm going for it once I come back around."

"All right, if you..."

"All units, Control. Calling on suit frequency." An unwelcome interruption. What can they add at this point? "Six minutes until realignment. Over."

My heart pounds.

And his hatch comes into view and there he is, springing across the gap, golden visor getting larger in the window. I flinch involuntarily; there is a thud, off to the side.

"You've got it!"

"Moving toward your hatch. I am..." (Grunting, straining on the radio.) "No, coming off."

"No!"

"Four minutes to realignment."

And as his spacecraft tumbles I see the tether looped around the Lunar Craft like fishing line on a reel, drawing him in tighter as the dead craft rotates, and Blondie is pulling on it, fighting it, trying to keep from getting wrapped up in it, his transfer case tangled...

With nothing to do, I narrate. "It's looping around, it's pulling you back in."

"I'm well aware of that. I have to get...back around..." He gasps.

"Ditch the transfer case if you have to."

"Can you get in closer?"

"Is my back clear?"

"Yes, you've..." A grunt and a pause. "...you've got about five meters."

"All right, I can try." I'm strapped back in; I pulse the thrusters.

"Two minutes to realignment."

"All right. Trying again."

Strapped in, farther from the porthole now, I cannot see as much but I catch a glimpse of him coming again, the hook for the other tether in hand, the leash tighter now, and he comes to the end and it is not enough, he stops midway and is pulled backwards by his tether as his ship tumbles, and then he's turned away. I can't see; I can't give advice.

"Getting tight here...the tether's wrapped around me... trying to get out from under it..." Heavy breathing now.

"Blondie, don't exert yourself. Your suit..." Another glimpse out the window and he is fighting, he is tangled up in the tether, tied up on the side of the Lunar Craft.

"Damnit, I..."

"All units, Control. Commencing realignment..."

"NO! Stop." I mash the button to terminate the groundlink. "He isn't on yet. We have to push it. He isn't on yet."

"Eagle-2, we can't push it much. -1, how soon can you get there?"

"I'm going to have to…" (Grunting, heavy breathing.) "…I have to unclip. Boris, I have to push off the ship. You'll have to come get me."

I eye the thrusters. Will it be enough? It doesn't matter. "Copy, Blondie. Just…get away from the Lunar Craft."

"Put the orbital module straight down at the moon."

"That angle won't work for the screen."

"There's more to grab this way." More heavy breathing. "Just…don't use the thrusters until I say."

"How can I maneuver without…"

"After that's done! Once I'm close, once I'm on, don't use them then!"

I picture the thruster firing: flame on the suit, rapid decompression. "All right. Maneuvering now." I pulse the thrusters, translate above him, rotate into position; I can see the moon stretching out in all directions, moving fast past us; now with the window angle I can barely catch glimpses of the edge of his spaceship as it tumbles. There are snippets on the rendezvous screen, flashing in front of the televised moon, but I'm basically blind. "All right, how's that?"

"It will have to do. Coming over now. And…"

I can't see. It kills me. I wait for the thud. But there is no thud.

"I missed it." Breathing softer now: he is floating free. But still panting, catching his breath. "You're going to have to rotate."

Three axes, no directions. "Rotate how?"

"Forty-five degrees plus-y."

"Are you clear of my thrusters?"

A pause. "Yes, clear."

"All right. Rotating now." On screen now, nothing but black-and-white moon. Through the window I glimpse a line of tether. Is he still hooked to something?

"And translate now. Again in the..."

Control steps on the transmission. "All units, how soon can we align? Over."

"JUST WAIT A GODDAMN MINUTE, CONTROL! Blondie, what direction?"

"Plus-y. Just nudge it forward a couple meters."

"I'm not going to hit your ship, am I?"

"No, no."

"You're sure?"

"I'm sure." He breathes, somehow relaxed now. "Plus-y. Just a pulse."

And I breathe.

Just a pulse.

The spaceship moves, and there is a small tremor, and I know he is on.

Again his voice, tired and soothing. "There we go."

Control tiptoes back in to the conversation. "All units, how soon can we realign?"

Blondie: "Give me a minute, Control. I need to get inside. Over."

Key the mike: "Blondie, you don't need me to maneuver?"

"No, you're good now." A few deep breaths. "I'm too close to the thrusters anyway."

And I take my hands off the controls, and I can still see a loop of the tether out of the porthole, and I unstrap to get closer and see what he could possibly still be attached to, and it is...the transfer case. That magnificent son of a whore still brought over the transfer case.

"Coming up on the hatch now."

"It will be good to see your face, Blondie." I think I really mean it.

"One thing, before I crack it open..."

"Anything, Blondie."

"Have you closed the internal hatch?"

And I look up at the wide round opening leading to the orbital module, and imagine the rush of air, the cyclone of paper, the vacuum of space sucking breath from my lungs. I imagine it, and smile tiredly.

"That would probably be a good idea."

•••

And now he is there on the other side of the hatch, and the indicator lights are on, and the orbital module is pressurizing. And we have missed the burn.

"Control, Eag...excuse me, Golden Eagle. I am ready to do a manual burn. Over." My hands hover near the controllers. I can save this, if they let me.

The answer takes its time. "Golden Eagle, Control. Negative on the manual burn. We will not be able to do another near-side firing. Given the computing times, the BESM-6 will need to calculate return-to-earth parameters based on your current orbit. Over."

I move my hands away. "Copy, Control." What else can I say?

"It's going to be a long low flight around the far side. If you make it. Over."

"At least we'll both be here for it, Control."

A wait while they think. "We still need to do a 106-K alignment now. Before we lose sunlight."

I reconnect the groundlink. "Do whatever you'd like, Control." I look down at the lengthening shadows, the first rays of Copernicus, with the crater itself invisible now beyond the shortened horizon, just like Langrenus was. My three craters are far behind us now; I had not even thought to look for them. I will never see them again like I did.

Blondie's spaceship tumbles in the distance, abandoned and alone, tether looped around like yarn. That at least is a new sight.

I watch the gauges as the pressure climbs. I stare at the hatch, the big ring of the latch. Despite everything else, he is there on the other side. He is right there, soon to be breathing my air. And none of the rest of it matters.

And when the hatch opens he is there floating, visor open but still in the moon suit, face still a little red, glistening with layers of sweat that cling to it strangely in weightless space.

And now the thrusters are pulsing, the spacecraft aligning itself under Control's guiding hand so the big sensor can catch the sun before it dips over the hostile horizon. Blondie and I both brace ourselves against the motion; his hands grab the hatch while his body floats free, legs swaying with every firing.

He smiles. "Smooth as a peeled egg."

I float up and clap him on the shoulder, then surprise myself, and him, by kissing the top of his beautiful balding head. Sweat be damned.

He smirks. "That could not have been pleasant."

"It was fine." I wipe his gross sweat from my lips. His spacesuit looks different somehow.

"Well rest assured, it is good to see you too."

I think again of closing the internal hatch, the catastrophe so narrowly averted. Then I realize why his suit looks strange: smudges of black on his knees, moon dust caked on his boots. We have done a lot more than just avert catastrophe. "You were down there! You were really down there!"

He laughs. "Where did you think I was?"

"Well, I...nothing, nevermind."

"What, Boris?"

"It occurred to me before the landing that you could have...I don't know. Hung out in a low orbit. Faked the transmissions."

A strange look. "I would have had a radio blackout every orbit. Don't you think Control would have noticed? Said something?"

"I mean...not if they were in on it."

He laughs. "Now you're talking crazy!" A clap on my shoulder, a comradely gesture. "Maybe you are a Great Russian after all!"

And in that sentence I hear its silent reverse, its far side— the word that is the other half of me, as far as most Russians can see. After all this, that.

I float back a little, eye him from a distance. "Maybe you crushed up your artist's charcoal. Smeared it on your suit."

His face scrunches, an exaggerated sniff. "Do you smell that, Comrade Volynov? Smell that! Does that smell like artist's charcoal?"

I sneeze. It does feel like I have hay fever, all of the sudden.

He goes on. "That is the smell of dust that's never been exposed to air. Coarse dust, never subject to erosion. We are the first humans to ever smell that smell."

"If you say so." Again I sneeze. "I don't know what it smells like, exactly."

He nods towards the inner hatch, the transfer case floating behind him in the orbital module, untethered now. "That's why I brought that. We've got rocks!"

"As if the KGB couldn't have...made some pad technician smuggle a case full of rocks on board your ship before you lifted off."

"We've got pictures!"

And I see the camera, clipped to his waist; I can't help but be amazed that the son of a whore still had the presence of mind to grab it, with everything else happening. "If you say so!"

And I sneeze, again and again and again.

•••

We are both exhausted. But there are many things still undone, many items that must be checked off the list if we are to get out of this alive. And time is still finite: perhaps forty-five minutes.

I undo the latches on his life support pack so he can climb out the back of his spacesuit. I am the only other human who will see it caked in moon dust.

As he climbs out, I grab the transfer case to stow it in the descent module. It has mass; it is real. I am eager to see the contents, although it occurs to me that I won't do so until we're back home, assuming all goes well. His camera, too—he unclips that and pushes it and it tumbles like an asteroid. I grab it and stow it.

Now he is out of the suit; he could probably leave it floating free in the orbital module, but he stows it carefully, folds the arms lovingly. And I catch him giving a long glance out the window towards his dead empty spacecraft; he kisses his fingers and places them on the glass before floating into the descent module.

I am unfastening the toilet contraption when the call comes in. "Golden Eagle, Control. We have the calculations from the BESM-6 and are ready to program your homecoming burn. Over."

"Yes, Control, that would be a good next step!"

And they transmit, and I copy it all down just to make sure, all those wonderful grease-pencil numbers.

At last we are ready to close the interior hatch. I know I'll miss the extra space; I take a long lingering look around before leaving, spinning to catch anything we might have missed. There will be no going back to the room to pick up forgotten items.

"Golden Eagle, we are coming up on blackout. Please confirm orbital module separation. Over."

"Wait one, Control." I float through the hatch, join Leonov in the descent module, our home for the next three days.

With the inner hatch closed and him next to me, it feels even more cramped.

"No need to strap in yet," Leonov says. "Just make sure you press the right buttons."

"Oh! You want me to keep us alive! That hadn't occurred to me." As much sarcasm as I can muster. "I know my way around this spacecraft, believe me." Still I pause above the buttons. If I press the wrong ones and separate the instrument module, it will kill us. Not right away, but slowly, over the next few days, another Apollo 8...

"Well get on with it, then."

And I press, and there is the shudder of the pyrocartridges like God's hammer breaking our spacecraft apart. If it doesn't separate, will the burn home even work? Probably not, the mass will be all wrong.

But I look through the porthole, craning my neck, smearing the glass with forehead grease, and I can see that it *has* separated; I can see its dim shape blotting out the stars, lit ever so softly by the Earth. A small metal moon orbiting the real one, for a little while, at least.

Then it goes dark.

"Orbital module separated," I say out of reflex, although Control can't hear us now.

•••

Of course, everything will still mean nothing if the engine doesn't fire properly. Or if our orbit is too low to get to that point: we are skimming the mountains of the moon, far below anything we'd ever planned.

"Might as well strap in now," Leonov says, and does so.

"I don't want to get too comfortable." I stifle a yawn. It will be almost two in the morning when it happens. "At least one of us needs to be awake for it."

"Assuming we get there!" He smiles. "Look how high those mountains are!"

Outside the window, darkness below the firmament. A scene I've already seen, although of course it feels different, having to share it. "It looks like it did last orbit."

"I could have sworn I saw stars passing behind the mountains."

"Where?" Again I strain at the glass, imagining I can see our fate.

"Over here on my side." He smiles. "Just a second ago. You must have missed it."

I shake my head. I don't know what to believe. The first man on the moon is fucking around with me, just because he can.

"Think of it this way," he goes on. "You could be the first human to end up on the far side!"

There is a delay receiving the transmission, or deciphering it. My tired computer at last spits out its result. "Not if I have to share the record."

I scan the grease-pencil numbers once more. I confirm that everything was transmitted properly, that everything is displaying correctly.

The timer counts slowly. I slap my face to stay awake.

"In all seriousness, Boris. I was wrong about you. For many years I was wrong. You are quite the pilot. I am glad you made it up here."

My tired head nods, registering the compliment. Then I process the meaning beneath: Korolev's golden boy. Blondie—Leonov. Surely his recommendations carried a lot of weight. My real enemy is here before me. And I was right to hate him all these years.

"Was it because I'm a Jew?" I turn to face him. "Or because I'm me?"

"Would that be a more acceptable answer?"

In truth I do not know.

"Anyway," he goes on. "The past is the past. As I said before, you're with me now."

His words are no comfort. And I wonder if they will still be true in three days. But there is no point thinking about that now. We will have the rest of our lives to discuss this. Assuming we survive the next few minutes.

I strain at the glass. Look to the dark horizon, trying to spot stars eclipsed by mountains. But the angle is all wrong to see our future. I turn the periscope screen on: a dark circle of nothing. Only then do I finally strap in.

Again I slap my face. The timer moves slowly. But it moves.

A blast of sunlight, a view of the far side: the last. For now. I'll see it again in a year or two. If I come back.

When the timer is up, the engine fires, smooth and steady. A gentle hand shepherding us home.

•••

Time starts skipping; sleep steals scenes. Still I fight to stay awake. Not just to see one more (last?) earthrise—though there is that, and it means something new now—but to talk to Control.

"...den Eagle, Control. Come in. Over."

Their words jerk me awake; I realize I missed it.

"Control, Golden Eagle." Groggily I survey the small module; Leonov is fast asleep. "We are here. Over."

The delay jars my mind. At last: "Golden Eagle, can you give us a status? Over."

"Control, the engine fired successfully. And all systems are running smoothly. And we will see you in three days. But for now we need some rest. Over."

After the delay: a noise. It takes a moment to register: applause. Whatever issues we'd had during ascent and rendezvous, all is forgotten, or at least forgiven. "Copy, Golden Eagle. You've certainly earned it! Over."

Tiredly I recall that I need to place the spacecraft in its thermal control roll; if I don't do that now, they'll wake me in a few minutes to tell me. But first I look at the gauges. Just enough, just enough. I twist my right hand, yaw the spacecraft so the porthole points in the same direction we are flying. Leonov stirs but I do not wake him: I want to be alone for this.

And Earth is above the horizon, above it by a fair margin; already the moonscape is looking slightly different, slightly distant. The scene is not as expected, but I see that it is good.

I turn my spacecraft perpendicular to the sun's blinding rays, and I start the rotation, and I place the covers over the windows. Then I sign off with Control, my final duty done for the day. At last I can rest.

•••

In the morning I awaken to the same scene.

For a couple confused moments I think of Union-2: the view that I thought would be the last of my life is now recreated before me. Another descent module, another exterior hatch that used to be an interior one. But no, this is new: all is pristine and undamaged. And everything that happened yesterday has, in fact, still happened. I have a vision that the rest will go smoothly; we'll reenter in three days and the pyrocartridges will work fine this time. Although you never really know until it's over...

Leonov slumbers next to me. My enemy, although I suppose we'll have to pretend otherwise, for a few months at least. I envision motorcades, cheering crowds, bigger than for Yuri even. Will they put us together in one car, to acknowledge the realities of the mission? Or: separate cars, with me in the first to warm up the people, and him in the second to bask in their full adulation? I see benefits to either arrangement.

Aware now of my swelling bladder, I look around for the toilet contraption. In our haste and tiredness last night we had not hooked it up to the smaller wall valve the designers had crammed into this module. And now of course the lack of preparation is biting me in the ass; I struggle to get it connected, hoping all the while that Leonov will stay asleep and Control will give me a few more moments of solitude.

Alas, no. I insert myself into the apparatus safely, but once I turn on the vacuum motor, he starts stirring. And I am still finishing my business when the radio crackles to life.

"Golden Eagle, Control. Good morning! We can see that you're up and ready to start your day. Over."

I am aware, suddenly, of the electrodes that have been stuck to my chest since launch, my heart rate transmitted live to some panel in front of some junior flight controller with nothing to do this morning other than alert his team lead when we start moving. "Control, Golden Eagle. Somewhat ready. Over."

"Well the world is ready for you! They are still celebrating out in the streets. It is quite the party, believe me!"

"I'm sorry I'm missing it." The conversation has interrupted my concentration, halted my flow; I struggle to throw the mental switches.

They still don't get it. "Golden Eagle, we're picking up some…loud background noises. We do not copy. Over."

"I'M SORRY I'M MISSING IT!" I refuse, on principle, to turn off the apparatus before I'm done. "I'm busy with some...pressure relief. Over."

"Golden Eagle, speaking of pressure..." (It is noticeable already, the slivers of time being shaved from the communications delay.) "...we need a stir of your oxygen tanks to get an accurate reading. Over."

"Copy, Control." No rest. I suddenly recall horror stories from Yuri about people following him into bathrooms and attempting conversations at the urinal, or talking over the dividers if he opted for the stall; I shudder at the realization that I'll have no time to myself for the foreseeable future.

I finish at last, and of course Leonov is now fully awake; he'll surely be more cursed than me in that regard. He rubs the sleep from his eyes and floats around me to do his morning business as I stir the oxygen tanks.

"You'd think they'd realize," he says. "Biologically, you'd think they'd realize what everyone does first thing in the morning."

"I doubt anyone will ever again realize you need time for bodily functions. Gods don't take bathroom breaks."

"I'm still a man, Boris."

"Try telling them that." A nod toward the waiting world. "Mark my words, you'll be reminding people for the rest of your life." A strange curse. Perhaps I did get the better end of the bargain after all...

I start retrieving food packets as Leonov cleans his hands; I realize I have not done the same. Fortunately he doesn't notice.

As we float and eat our dehydrated breakfast meat I find myself eyeing the box of lunar rocks, so miraculously saved from rejoining their fellows on the moon; I glance at the dusty camera stowed behind my couch. We were too preoccupied last night to talk about his experience. I am reluctant to bring it up. But as we eat, the unspoken question swells to fill the silence. Is he going to force me to ask it?

"Should be a quiet day today," I observe.

"Hopefully." His eyes sparkle with secrets.

I sigh. "So...what was it like?"

"What was *what* like?" A grin.

"Oh, come on!" After all I did for him, surely I'm entitled to some details.

"It was something," he says at last. "It was really something."

"I'm sure it was." I eye the camera. That at least has answers.

"I did see the most incredible thing when I was down there," he goes on. "Just...really incredible. I didn't want to talk about it on the radio."

"Did you get pictures?"

"I..." A slow smile spreads. "Of course I got pictures. I took..." Wheels turn behind his eyes, some mysterious calculation. "...I took, what did I take? Four rolls of film."

"Four rolls." I do not know how to interpret any of this. "Well? What was it? This incredible thing?"

"It was half-buried in the dust, a few hundred meters from the lander." (His tone: dead serious.) "I thought I could see what it was as I walked up, but I didn't say anything on the airwaves." (Against my will, I'm hooked.) "I didn't want to sound like an idiot if I was wrong, but...I was not wrong. I wanted to bring back proof...it's in there." A nod towards the camera or the transfer case—I can't tell which. "I was not wrong, Boris." He pauses, looks me in the eyes, waits. Waits and waits and waits.

"Well?"

"It was a door. A door to a massive, buried alien structure." He holds the stone face for a few seconds, sober and serious, reliable as a statue...and then bursts into laughter.

"Blondie!"

"I almost had you! I need to practice. Maybe I can pull it off down there. If you're next to me, looking serious? Maybe nodding here and there..."

"Maybe." I shake my head. Will I do that, for him? I remember again the years of not flying, all the bitter disappointments; I have to remind myself to hate him. "But really, though. What did you see?"

"I saw…" (A deep breath.) "I saw Tom Stafford. Lying there, collapsed. There were footprints, a long line of footprints stretching back to the east, as far as the eye could see…" A serious stare; it is perhaps easier for him to keep a straight face with this story.

"Blondie."

"I'm sorry. That one's not…" He shakes his head: something like shame. "That is…" A deep breath as he looks off into the distance. Eyes glistening: tears? "I will say. Somehow his name always sounded…important to me. Even before the accident, it sounded important. Like we were meant to meet. Then when I was down there, back outside the lander, and the air in my suit was getting thick…" He leaves the rest unsaid, except for another shake of the head, and maybe I know what he means. Maybe.

I nod as if I do, and finish my food in silence.

"I'm sorry." He places his hand on my shoulder. "You really want to know what it was like?"

I'm sure my eyes betray me with an unspoken yes.

"It was like a dirty beach," he says. "Like an empty dirty beach. Some…barren wasteland outside a factory, coated in soot. A lot of emptiness, a lot of nothing."

I listen and nod, just a little; I picture it in my mind, the lander in that empty place, alone. Then I wind back through the transcripts in my mind and… "I thought you said you landed in a crater."

He gives a little smile; he smiles a little and says nothing.

I pull the covers from the windows. Outside again: blackness and sun. Nothing we haven't seen before.

I realize I need to stow my trash; I float around him to do so, and there it is, his camera, abraded by moon dust.

He is busy retrieving something from the other side of the capsule, but when he looks up, he can see what I'm looking at. "Oh!" Surprise. Then: a mischievous grin? "Can you get the film from that? There's some good stuff on there. I rewound it, but I didn't have time to remove the roll."

I have no accounting for my next action. Anger, apathy, stupidity, spite? (And no clear memory either. Or do I just want a secret of my own?) All I will say is that when I look down, the back of the camera is open, and he has in fact not rewound the film; I can see the bare celluloid, blasted with sunlight. I close the back slowly, knowing those pictures are ruined.

He sees what has happened. And am I imagining, or does he give a little nod? "Actually..." he says, still with the small smile, "...maybe I hadn't rewound it after all."

I shake my head, take a deep breath.

He purses his lips strangely; his eyes narrow. Calculation or memory? "Come to think of it...those other three rolls of film I took? I think I may have left them."

"Left them?"

"In the pockets of the moon suit."

"Oh." The suit that is now tucked away in the orbital module, thousands of kilometers behind us.

"I'm not sure." Again a smile. "It was a hectic evening."

Is he fucking around with me again? Did he pocket the film when he thought I wasn't looking? I scan the fading scenes but find no answers, nothing reliable; the pictures are all melted together in memory. Anger rises, more real now. I choke it down. Three more days of this...is it possible we can share this space in peace, for the little time we have left?

There is nothing in the spacecraft to see, nothing we haven't already seen, but he is there with the tools of the artist. He straps back in and pauses, sketchpad on his lap, charcoal poised above the blank space. "Don't worry, though, Boris. I'll still put in a good word for you with Kamanin. And who knows?" A nod towards the useless camera and its ruined film. "Maybe I'll even say I did that."

And I can envision it, him in a room, speaking to others about me, without me. What do I want him to say? Do I want another trip? I can't have the one he had; I'd be going elsewhere, and mine would be mine anyway. It might be nice just to have this one; I was part of this, after all, and this will be the one people care about. Although of course it would also be nice to see for myself what it's like down there...but could I enjoy the scene, knowing I was in it? Knowing how little certainty there is in the return? Could I enjoy it before I was back on Earth, before I knew the ending?

I imagine the pictures, the ones I'll see weeks from now, or never, the ones either hiding in his pocket as part of an impromptu prank, or circling the moon in our discarded module. I look over at his drawing, the lines he's set down so far: the round frame of the lander window, and a horizon through the middle. He sees me watching, and looks down, and frowns; he tears the sheet out, crumples it up. And he pauses for a moment over the next blank page— remembering or imagining, I can't tell. And he sets down a series of circles. Circles and circles and circles.

I watch in silence as he completes the picture. And I wonder if I'll ever know for sure.

Acknowledgments

I could not have written this series alone, and couldn't have found readers without great help from others in the space writing community. In particular I would like to thank Francis French, a talented writer, conscientious researcher, generous reader, and all-around class act. Emily Carney is another very conscientious researcher and writer whose great enthusiasm for the series has helped pull me along; she's also tireless in debunking spaceflight myths, and fostering a healthy and welcoming online community at *Space Hipsters* on Facebook. David Hitt—author of the definitive book on the Skylab missions—has also been very kind with his time and reading and blurbs. And Martin Seay, while not a space writer, has been an excellent and generous blurbist and friend, whose insights I value greatly.

I'm tremendously grateful to Giano Cromley for his friendship, and his editing and feedback; he caught several boneheaded mistakes in my writing. Any remaining errors are mine alone.

I've been drawn to space writing in part because it makes plotting simple—your mission is your story—and to historical writing because there's no need to come up with characters. Putting Alexei Leonov as the first Soviet man on the moon was a no-brainer; I've never heard any other cosmonaut mentioned as a contender. Plus, there were plenty of English-language resources about him, including his enjoyable joint autobiography with Dave Scott, *Two Sides of the Moon*. I hope I've been fair in fictionalizing him.

Picking a second crewmember was tougher, particularly when the muses told me I needed to tell the story through his eyes. I first read about Boris Volynov's harrowing Soyuz-4 descent in Francis French and Colin Burgess's excellent *In the Shadow of the Moon*, but I didn't realize I wanted him on my mission until I noticed his birthday was December 18th—a date that, for personal reasons, means a lot to me. Still I did not know much about him. Bert Vis graciously shared with me his research and thoughts on Volynov, and the character I have drawn here—prickly, somewhat mistrustful of judgments other than his own, eager to correct others—is largely based on my interpretation of Bert's interview with Volynov in May, 2001. As with Leonov, I hope I've been fair in my depiction.

Stephen Walker also graciously provided me with interview material that greatly fleshed out my understanding of Volynov; it contained valuable anecdotes from his life, and plenty of material that buttressed my initial impressions. (His book *Beyond* is an excellent chronicle of Yuri Gagarin's spaceflight, and a fascinating look at the Soviet program. I also strongly recommend *Shockwave*, his harrowing account of the atomic bombing of Japan.) I'm tremendously grateful as well for the advance read.

Even after all the research I still had no small amount of trepidation about writing a story through the eyes of a half-Jewish Soviet cosmonaut. Eager to get a better handle on the Soviet Jewish experience in the twentieth century, I asked Dmitry Samarov (who was born into a Soviet Jewish family at about the time of this manuscript, and lived in Moscow for the first few years of his life) for reading suggestions; he unhesitatingly recommended Vasily

Grossman's *Life and Fate*. It's a magnificent work that's starting to get some recognition but is still shamefully under-read; it's a World War II *War and Peace* written by someone who actually lived it. I can't thank Dmitry enough for recommending it; it undoubtedly influenced my final manuscript.

Since I'm talking influences, I should also mention *Meiselman* by Avner Landes, which I had the good fortune to publish; Avner's effortless depictions of his character's flights of fancy and dread undoubtedly helped shape my own efforts, which I can only hope were half as enjoyable. You should check out his book. (And I'm not just saying that because I'm making money off of it.)

My good friend and neighbor Yuriy Reznik offered valuable insights on Soviet culture and thought during our long walks around Rogers Park. He also recommended Yuri Slezkine's *The Jewish Century*, an insightful intellectual survey of the twentieth-century Jewish experience.

Asif Siddiqi remains the best all-around historian of the Soviet space program; I finally read *The Red Rockets' Glare: Spaceflight and the Soviet Imagination 1857-1957* when working on this, and his thoroughly researched work offered invaluable insights on the development of Soviet rocketry, and its role in the nation's collective consciousness. (His *Sputnik and the Soviet Space Challenge* and *The Soviet Space Race with Apollo* are also essential for anyone interested in Soviet spaceflight; I consulted them both while writing this.) I greatly appreciate his kind words both on this and on *Public Loneliness.*

In 2016 I had the good fortune of meeting Apollo 11's Michael Collins, a humble man who's now one of my personal heroes; he's gone now but lives on not only in his considerable accomplishments, and his wonderful family, but also in his magnificent book *Carrying the Fire*. It was a huge help in depicting this moon voyage; not only is it one of the best space memoirs I've read, it's one of the best memoirs, period. Be Thou At Peace, General Collins.

Jeffrey Kluger's *Apollo 8* was another great read for background information on lunar missions, with a wealth of detailed information.

I stumbled across *For the Moon and Mars N-1: A Reference Guide to the Soviet Superbooster* on Kickstarter, and it was a great resource on spacecraft geometry and features for the LK and LOK, as well as the timeframe and profile for a lunar landing mission. Big thanks to Matthew Johnson, Nick Stevens, Alexander Shliadinsky, Igor Bezyaev, Vladimir Antipov, and Jack Hagerty for putting it together. Even bigger thanks are due to Jack for putting me in touch with Alexander, and to Alexander for permission to use his line drawing.

Massive thanks to the multi-talented Michael Mackowski for permission to use his Soyuz 7K-OK line drawing on short notice.

Soyuz: A Universal Spacecraft by Rex D. Hall and David J. Shayler was a very handy reference guide any time I had questions about interior spacecraft geometry.

I based the final LK descent profile on a graphic (© 1999 by Mark Wade) posted at http://astronautix.com/graphics/l/lkprof.gif

Anatoly Zak's website www.russianspaceweb.com remains indispensable for anyone doing research on the Soviet and Russian space programs; it provided much useful information on the LK lander, the Block-E stage, and the various spacesuits that would have been used.

James R. Hansen's *First Man: The Life of Neil A. Armstrong* is an excellent treatment of its subject, and helped me think of several things I needed to include in this manuscript.

I read *Aelita* by Alexei Tolstoy and *Red Star* by Alexander Bogdanov; both offered valuable insights into Russian utopianism towards space travel.

I'd wanted to visit Moscow before I wrote this; a couple factors (failing to get an applied-for grant, travel restrictions brought on by the COVID epidemic) made it clear that wouldn't happen. Hopefully Google Street View allowed for at least some realism in my depictions of the Kremlin.

It's a great time to be alive for anyone doing historical research on the filmed portions of the twentieth century; the YouTube video "Travelling to Moscow ft. Sir Laurence Olivier, Robert Lang, & More (1965) | British Pathé" posted on April 13, 2014 was essential in getting a glimpse of mid-60s Moscow. You can view it at: https://youtu.be/8uK5y8YjJTM

The video "Ordinary life in the USSR 1961" was also helpful. URL: https://www.youtube.com/watch?v=ExHCAjRsZhA

Several videos in the YouTube channel "SOVIET SPACE PROGRAM (Космическая программа СССР)" provided great historical information, particularly "Восход-1 Voskhod

1 1964." URL: https://www.youtube.com/watch?v=qcM1QLxIUew

Vladimir Motyl's *White Sun of the Desert* (the movie everyone launching on a Soyuz has watched for good luck since the early 1970s) is quite a hoot.

The YouTube video "Horizons mission - Soyuz: launch to orbit" posted on June 25, 2018 by the European Space Agency is an excellent crew-cabin view of the launch of a Soyuz capsule, and was a great aid in depicting the launch of the fictional Union-2. URL: https://www.youtube.com/watch?v=fr_hXLDLc38

The YouTube video "Soyuz undocking, reentry and landing explained" posted on November 11, 2013 by the European Space Agency had some great explanation, narration, and footage related to Soyuz reentry and descent, and was also a big help in depicting Union-2. URL: https://www.youtube.com/watch?v=-I7MM9yoxII

I downloaded Virtual Moon Atlas 7.0 by Christian Legrand and Patrick Chevalley and used it very frequently; it was an essential resource on lunar geography.

The phone app "Moon Atlas 3D" was also a very handy reference for geography and lunar features.

The Lunar and Planetary Institute's lunar distance calculator and the spherical geometry equations on Wikipedia's "Horizon" page were both invaluable in determining what an orbiting cosmonaut would see at various altitudes; the LPI's calculator is located at https://www.lpi.usra.edu/lunar/tools/lunardistancecalc/

And if anyone is interested in the story of the six lunar landings we've had so far, *A Man on the Moon* by Andrew Chaikin is a must-read—authoritative, detailed, excellently written. It's easily in my all-time top five nonfiction books. Please do check it out.

About the Author

Gerald Brennan earned a B.S. in European History from the United States Military Academy at West Point and an M.S. in Journalism from Columbia University in New York. He's the author of *Resistance*, as well as four space books including *Island of Clouds*, which Neal Thompson said was "Speculative sci-fi at its finest." He's also the founder of Tortoise Books, a Chicago-based independent press; *Newcity* named him to their 2019 Lit 50 list of notable literary Chicagoans, and noted Chicago journalist Rick Kogan called the press "...one of the best, most provocative, and rewarding publishing houses in the entire country."

Follow him on Twitter: @jerry_brennan.

About Tortoise Books

Slow and steady wins in the end, even in publishing. Tortoise Books is dedicated to finding and promoting quality authors who haven't yet found a niche in the marketplace—writers producing memorable and engaging works that will stand the test of time.

Learn more at www.tortoisebooks.com or follow us on Twitter: @TortoiseBooks.

CPSIA information can be obtained
at www.ICGtesting.com
Printed in the USA
JSHW052309060522
25711JS00004B/4

9 781948 954653